"I'm looking forward to..."

He could no longer resist her cherry pink lips, and his mouth claimed hers in a sweet, gentle kiss. When she did not pull away, he allowed his kiss to deepen. The feelings that flooded over him were a total surprise. He had never felt quite like this before. These were not the kind of feelings the guys at the gym talked about when they discussed the women in their lives. These were weird and wonderful feelings. Feelings of love and passion and, yes, even protectiveness. He wanted to scoop her up in his arms and carry her off to some faraway island where she could be his alone, without the pressures of everyday life and the demands of the world. *What am I doing, holding her and kissing her like this?* He backed away slightly and tried to shake such foolish thoughts from his brain. Other than the job she performed each day for him and singing in the cantata, they had practically nothing in common. Not only that, but she was a devout Christian. Her whole life centered on God. He did not even believe in God!

JOYCE LIVINGSTON has done many things in her life (in addition to being a wife, mother of six, and grandmother to oodles of grand-kids, all of whom she loves dearly), from being a television broadcaster for eighteen years, to lecturing and teaching on quilting and sewing, to writing magazine articles on a variety of subjects. She's danced with Lawrence Welk, ice-skated with a chimpanzee, had bottles broken over her head by stuntmen, interviewed hundreds of celebrities and controversial figures, and done many other interesting and unusual things. But now, when she isn't off traveling to wonderful and exotic places as a part-time tour escort, her days are spent sitting in front of her computer, creating stories. She feels her writing is a ministry and a calling from God, and she hopes Heartsong readers will be touched and uplifted by what she writes. Joyce loves to hear from her readers and invites you to visit her on the Internet at www.joycelivingston.com.

Books by Joyce Livingston

HEARTSONG PRESENTS
HP353—Ice Castle
HP602—Dandelion Bride
HP382—The Bride Wore Boots
HP618—One Last Christmas
HP437—Northern Exposure
HP482—Hand Quilted with Love
HP516—Lucy's Quilt
HP521—Be My Valentine
HP546—Love Is Kind
HP566—The Baby Quilt
HP578—The Birthday Wish

Don't miss out on any of our super romances. Write to us at the following address for information on our newest releases and club information.

Heartsong Presents Readers' Service
PO Box 719
Uhrichsville, OH 44683

Or visit www.heartsongpresents.com

Down from the Cross

Joyce Livingston

Heartsong Presents

To my dear husband, Don Livingston, who is also my number one fan. Of all the books I have written, this one—*Down from the Cross*—is his favorite. Two months ago, Don was diagnosed with brain cancer and underwent surgery to remove a golf ball–sized tumor. Things looked bleak. On his way to the hospital, he turned and with tears in his eyes said he wanted the Lord to allow him to live long enough to hold the published book in his hands. You see, he is in this writing ministry with me. Each time one of my books is released, Don purchases a number of copies and mails them to family, friends, and those he wants to see accept Christ as their Savior. He believed so strongly in the message of *Down from the Cross*, he wanted to live long enough to share it with a long list of people, many who are in the public eye. As I write this dedication, Don is still with me. God willing, he will live long enough to meet his goal. I love him dearly and cannot imagine life without him. Please pray for us.

A note from the Author:
I love to hear from my readers! You may correspond with me by writing:

Joyce Livingston
Author Relations
PO Box 719
Uhrichsville, OH 44683

ISBN 1-59310-261-5

DOWN FROM THE CROSS

Our mission is to publish and distribute inspirational products offering exceptional value and biblical encouragement to the masses.

All scripture quotations are taken from the King James Version of the Bible.

All of the characters and events in this book are fictitious. Any resemblance to actual persons, living or dead, or to actual events is purely coincidental.

PRINTED IN THE U.S.A.

Or check out our Web site at www.heartsongpresents.com

one

Keene Moray loved Providence, Rhode Island. If he could choose one place in the lower forty-eight to live on a permanent basis, it would be Providence, right in the heart of the New England area. Unfortunately, his profession required him to live elsewhere—in New York City—but not by choice. It wasn't that he didn't love the Big Apple. He did. But it had become too crowded, too demanding, and far too busy for his liking.

"This is the city for me," he said aloud, flipping on his turn signal as he drove his new BMW convertible down Francis Street toward the convention center. "With its relaxed, laid-back atmosphere. Someday I'm going to have myself a house in this city. Maybe a lovely old brick mansion."

He sped up and then reached to insert a new CD into the player in the dash. It slipped from his fingers and fell onto the thickly carpeted floor. With a quick glance to check the traffic ahead of him, he bent to retrieve the elusive CD.

Suddenly his body lunged forward, only to be yanked back by the seat belt, the noise of crashing metal deafening his ears. The car's air bag pinned him against the seat back, and his head slammed into the headrest. The BMW filled with a misty gray haze from the air bag's powdery substance. Although the bag deflated instantly, Keene found it difficult to breathe. He instinctively yanked the buckle open on his seat belt, found the car door handle, and pushed open the door, staggering out in search of fresh air to fill his lungs.

That's when he fully realized what had happened.

❧

"Uggh!" Jane Delaney leaned her forehead against the steering wheel, her heart pounding erratically. *What happened? Why is that horn honking?* With trembling fingers, she reached for the knot forming on her forehead. "My car!" She pushed away and struggled to open the door, but the handle wouldn't budge. "Oh, dear Lord, I've been in an accident. Please, God, don't let my car be ruined!"

Though it hurt to move, she forced herself over the console and passenger seat, wincing at the stabbing pain in her left leg. She pushed her way out the door, nearly falling when she tried to stand to her feet. With the bright morning sun blinding her, she hobbled around the front of her car, placing her palms on the hood for support. She felt faint, light-headed, and woozy, and it scared her. She'd never felt this way before. However, her fright didn't compare with the feelings of helplessness and exasperation she experienced when she caught sight of the driver's side of her car. She stood staring, gaping at the damage, everything going in and out of focus.

A hand gripped her arm. "Are you all right? I am so sorry! I must've run a red light!" The man let his hold on her relax long enough to pull his cell phone from his belt. "I've got to call 911! You need an ambulance!"

❧

Keene grabbed for the woman, nearly dropping his phone, but despite his efforts she fell into a heap at his feet. "What have I done?" he shouted, quickly kneeing beside her and punching 911 into his phone. The dispatcher answered immediately.

"Help, someone, help! I've just run into a woman's car, and I think she's unconscious!"

"Give me your location, sir, and we'll have someone right

there," the dispatcher answered calmly with an authority that did nothing to calm Keene's frazzled nerves.

He looked around quickly, hoping to find a street sign or some other indication of his location. "I'm. . .I'm on Francis Street."

"Where on Francis Street, sir? Can you give me the name of a nearby cross street, maybe a familiar landmark?"

His mind raced. "I–I don't know. . .I was on Francis Street heading toward the convention center. . ." He paused, trying to remember what happened.

Several people were gathering now, one man bending over the young woman with great concern. Keene leaned toward him, his own breath coming in short gasps. "Where am I?"

Apparently familiar with the area, the man looked up and said, "Francis Street and Sabin."

"Francis Street and Sabin," Keene barked into the phone, relieved to be able to relay accurate information.

"Thank you, sir. They'll find you."

"Tell them to hurry, please. I don't know how badly she is hurt, but her head is bleeding. How could I have done this?"

"Ugghh."

Keene turned quickly at the sound. At least the woman was alive. He pulled a freshly ironed handkerchief from his pocket and pressed it to her forehead. If only he could stop the bleeding. "Hang on, lady. Help is coming. Someone should be here any minute." Blinking hard, he covered his face with his free hand. *How could this have happened? One minute I was driving along, putting a CD—the CD! It dropped onto the floor, and I reached for it! I didn't even see the woman's car!*

He scanned Francis Street in both directions for any sign of the emergency vehicle, his frantic gaze locking on the stoplight. *A stoplight! I ran a stoplight! I could have killed that woman!*

The wail of a siren brought him to his feet. Keene moved quickly out of the way yet stayed close enough to see and hear the things going on as an ambulance pulled up beside him, followed by a police car, then a fire engine.

"Can you tell me what happened, sir?" Clipboard in hand, the police officer hurriedly exited his car and began making notations.

"It was my fault!" Keene gestured toward the stoplight. "I—I didn't see the stoplight."

Poising his ballpoint pen over the clipboard, the officer took on a dubious expression. "I'll need your full name and address."

"My. . .my name is Keene Moray. M-O-R-A-Y. I'm staying at. . .at. . ." His mind went blank. "I'm staying at. . .at— oh, what is the name of that place?"

He described the complex where the condominium he had rented for the next few months was located, and fortunately, the officer recognized it by its description and came up with the name, Kennewick Place.

Keene nodded. "Do you think she's going to be all right?" He craned his neck over the crowd that had assembled, trying to get a glimpse of the woman when the EMTs lifted her onto the gurney.

The officer turned, looked briefly in her direction, and then continued writing. "Don't know. Sometimes these intersection collisions can do more serious damage to the drivers than to the cars." The officer stopped writing, his slight frown converting to one of understanding. "Hang on a minute, and I'll see what I can find out."

Keene watched as the man strode over to one of the EMTs, conversed with him for a second, jotted down a few notes, then walked back. The two stood watching the men loading the gurney into the waiting ambulance. Then the doors closed, and it headed back down the street, lights flashing.

"He said it didn't look like her injuries were life-threatening," the officer told him. "She probably fainted from the trauma of the accident and the loss of blood. That happens sometimes, especially if it's the person's first accident. However, they were concerned about her left ankle. They're taking her to the hospital to make sure she's all right and there are no internal injuries. Standard procedure for this type of thing." He let loose a slight chuckle. "Guess she gave them quite a battle. She didn't want to go to the hospital, kept saying she didn't have insurance and couldn't afford it."

Keene stared at the twisted wreckage of the woman's little economy car, then at his solid BMW. While her car looked to be a total loss, his had sustained only minor damage to the hood, bumper, and lights, and he felt terrible. "I'll pay for her hospital bill, and of course, I'll have her car repaired or replaced. It was my fault."

The officer peered over his sunglasses with a hint of a cautioning smile. "Don't think your lawyer would be happy hearing you say that. I'm going to have to give you a citation for running that red light, you know."

"Did you get her name?" The least of Keene's worries right now was the cost of the ticket he would have to pay. Without a doubt, he was the one who had caused the accident, and he would be more than willing to answer for his carelessness and irresponsibility. That poor woman! He could have killed her.

"Oh, yeah," the officer said, looking up from his book. "I got it. It's Jane Delaney."

❧

Jane winced and sighed in frustration. She had been in a hospital a number of times, but she had never been a patient.

"Well, how are we feeling?" A big-boned woman in a heavily

starched nurse's uniform came bustling into the cubicle. "You were pretty upset when they brought you in. You're looking a little better now."

How are we feeling? Jane wanted to smile at the woman's question, but her sore face would not allow it. Even the slightest movement hurt. Besides, she had more important things on her mind. Like how would she ever pay for all of this? She had not been able to make a car or insurance payment in over three months. A letter from the insurance company was sitting on her dresser right now, saying they had already canceled her. And what could she use for transportation now that one whole side of her car had caved in?

The nurse bent over her, tugging the cover up beneath her chin. "Are you hungry? It's nearly noon. I think I can get you a lunch tray. Yummy, yummy! Chicken noodle soup, celery sticks, cherry Jell-O, and chocolate pudding!"

"No, thank you. My. . .my stomach doesn't feel like food right now." Jane struggled to get comfortable on the narrow bed but winced when a sharp pain in her injured leg prevented it. "Ouch!"

"Oh, are we hurting?" The woman bustled around the bed, filling the water glass and straightening the side table.

I don't know about you, but I am! "A little, I guess. I've got to get out of here."

The woman gave her a pleasant smile. "You're not going anywhere until the doctor says you can. How's the head doing?" She bent to look more closely at the wound. "Umm, they did a good job putting those sutures in. Shouldn't leave too much of a scar. You're lucky that cut is in your hairline."

Jane's free hand went to her head. "I'm. . .I'm kind of light-headed. Dizzy. You know what I mean?"

The woman nodded. "I'm not surprised with a knot like

that. I'm amazed you don't have an unbearable headache." She quit her fussing and gave Jane a sudden frown. "You don't, do you?"

"Not really. It's not too bad. It's my leg that hurts." She scooted to the edge of the bed and slowly hung her legs over the side. "I—I have to go to the restroom."

"I brought you a walker. Do you think you can hobble to the bathroom by holding on to it?" The nurse took a firm grasp on her arm and tugged her forward. "By the way, my name's Mildred."

Warily, Jane slid one foot to the floor, placing a hand on the mattress to brace herself.

"Whoa, take your time, and let me keep a hold on you. I don't want you falling." The nurse grabbed on to the walker's handle grips. "Steady there. Get your bearings before you try to take any steps."

"Are you sure she should be out of bed?" an anxious-sounding male voice asked from the doorway.

Jane spun around, realizing too late she had moved more quickly than she should. She all but fell back into Mildred's arms.

The man rushed toward them, but Mildred shooed him off. "I've got her. She's fine." She helped Jane lower herself back onto the bed.

Jane clutched at the front of her hospital gown and scooted her hips back onto the mattress.

The man turned his head away, apparently realizing for the first time that he had invaded her privacy. "I'm. . .I'm so sorry," he stammered, looking every direction but at the two women. "It's just that I've been so worried about you. It seemed no one would tell me anything about your condition."

Jane eyed him inquisitively as she lay back down. He was a

handsome man, maybe ten years older than she, with dark, closely cropped hair, big brown eyes, and dark lashes. "Are. . . are you sure you're in the right place?"

"Oh, I'd recognize you anywhere."

His quick answer mystified her, yet after taking a second glance at him, she realized he did look vaguely familiar. Her mind raced to pull up his identity from the depths of her brain's database.

He hurried to the side of the bed, hovering over her like an overattentive mother. "I'm. . .I'm the one who put you here."

She instinctively pushed back into the pillow. "You work for the hospital? I'm sorry. I don't have insurance and I—"

He shook his head vehemently. "Oh, no. You have it all wrong. I—I ran the stoplight. I didn't mean to, really I didn't. I didn't see it. The sun. . .my car. . .the CD on the floor. . ."

What is he saying? Her muddled mind registered a big fat zero. His words made no sense at all.

"I didn't see you," he said, peeking around the nurse, "then suddenly I hit your car! I was so afraid, I mean. . .you were bleeding. . .I called 911. . .the officer wanted my address and I couldn't remember it."

Mildred took over. "Slow down, mister. I don't even have a knot on my head, and I have no idea what you're talking about. From the confused look on my patient's face, I'm sure she doesn't either." She sent a quick glance toward Jane.

He reached forward and grabbed on to Jane's arm. "Please, hear me out. I'm sorry for being so incoherent, but. . .but I've never injured anyone before."

Jane felt herself staring at the man as jagged pieces of her memory processed his words. "You're the one who hit me?"

He lowered his head and gnawed on his lower lip. "Yes, but

I intend to make things right with you. After all, it was my fault! I'd. . .I'd like to talk to you, if you feel up to it."

Mildred rolled her eyes and shook her head as she drew a chair up close to the bed and motioned him toward it. Then, wagging her finger in his face, she said, "I don't want you upsetting her, you hear? I'll be right here watching you."

He seemed relieved and moved into the chair. "Let me start at the beginning."

Jane looked from the stranger to Mildred and back to the stranger again. "I'm listening."

"I don't live in Providence," he began. "I live in New York City, but I'm making my residence here for the next few months." Seeming to weigh his words before saying them, he sucked in a deep breath and exhaled slowly. "I was driving on Francis Street near the convention center and was nearing the intersection when I decided to change CDs. But when I went to insert the new one in the CD player, it slipped from my fingers onto the floor. I checked the oncoming traffic then reached for it and. . ."

"That's when you hit me?" Jane shuddered, remembering the dreadful sound of the collision and the instant pain it had caused.

He nodded. "Yes. With the sun shining in my eyes when I looked up, I guess I didn't see the stoplight. All of a sudden, I felt myself being thrown forward and my air bag inflated. I never even saw your car before I hit you."

"I had the right of way! The light was green!" she nearly screamed at him. "Do you have any idea what you did to my car?"

The man closed his eyes tightly shut and shuddered. "Yes, I did see what I did to your car, and I'm so sorry. I can't begin to tell you how sorry."

Normally Jane was easygoing, but she felt her temper rising. A temper she did not even realize she had until a vision of her battered little car surfaced in her mind. "You wrecked my car! It's not even six months old. The first new car I've ever owned, and now I'll have to make payments on a car that probably won't even run!" Tears burst from her eyes.

"I'm sure your insurance would cover it, but don't worry about that." He leaned toward her, both hands gripping the edge of the mattress. "I plan to make amends. My insurance company will pay to have your car fixed, and if it can't be fixed, they'll replace it for you."

"And what about this?" She held out her battered leg, cringing with pain as she extended it. "I don't have a nickel's worth of insurance to cover the hospital costs."

"I'm sure my insurance will cover that, too, but if it doesn't, I will," he assured her once again. "Please don't be concerned about it. Things will work out."

She looked away from him and stared at the wall. "Don't be concerned about it? That's easy for you to say. You're not the one going through this!"

"I—I know, and I'm so sorry you have to go through this unexpected ordeal. I wish I could undo what happened, but I can't."

Her fingers rubbing at her temples, she let out a deep sigh. "You don't know the half of it, mister."

"I'm sure you're going to be greatly inconvenienced until your injuries heal, and I will be happy to do anything I can to help you. Anything."

He seemed sincere, but there was no way he could help her. Her injuries and the loss of her car were only the beginning. "Nothing you can do. Not really." She felt her chest heave up and down, the memory and magnitude of her problems nearly overwhelming her. "Only a miracle from God can help me now."

"I wouldn't expect anything like that if I were you," he said matter-of-factly, shrugging with a hopeless gesture.

Upset by his words, she gave him a cold stare. "Why? Why would you say such a thing? God can perform miracles. He's done it in my life many times."

His look was patronizing, and she resented both it and his implication that God could not answer prayer.

"I don't mean to upset you, Mrs. Delaney, but—"

"Miss. It's Miss Delaney."

"Like I said, I don't mean to upset you, Miss Delaney, but there is no scientific proof that there is a God."

Her dander rose at his words. "What a ridiculous thing to say, when there's so much evidence to the contrary!"

"As an educated man, I have no choice. I must bow to the scientific scholars."

"What do they know? How do they explain the miraculous birth of a baby, or the sun rising and setting at exact times, or like my father used to say—a black cow eating green grass and giving white milk and yellow butter?"

He sent a quick glance toward Mildred. "Look, Miss Delaney, I'm sorry. The last thing I want to do is upset you." His voice was soft and kind and seemed to bear no malice. "I should never have started our conversation this way. I merely meant you do not have to rely on some unknown God for a miracle. I ran the stoplight, I hit your car, and I'll gladly face up to my responsibilities and take care of all of it—your car, your hospital and doctor bills, and anything else you might need."

Balling her fists, she glared at him. "That's all well and good, but do you realize your carelessness has ruined my life?"

"Yes, I realize that, and all I can do is say I'm sorry and do the best I can to make up for it. I am a man of honor." He shifted nervously, rattling the change in his pocket. "I'm sorry about what I said. About your God. I didn't mean to offend you in any way."

His words about God *had* angered her, but his softened voice and apology helped soothe both her anger and frustration. However, she had to let this man, who appeared to have no financial problems at all, know what this accident had done to her already messed-up life. Stressed to the limit, she sucked in a deep breath and counted to ten before speaking through gritted teeth, enumerating her problems by counting them on her fingers. "I don't expect you to be interested, but my car and hospital bills are just the beginning of my problems. Two days ago, the company I have worked for the past twelve years told me they were going to cut back and lay off a number of their employees. I happened to be one of them. I am the caregiver to my aged, ailing mother, which keeps me from getting a second job even if I could find one. She needs medicine I can't afford to buy for her, the landlord just raised our rent five percent, and my beautiful cocker spaniel died last week of pneumonia. Now do you see why I am upset? Tell me what you're going to do about *those* things?"

He gave her an incredulous look. "Even if there is a God, I'm not sure even *He* could take care of all those things to your satisfaction. That's a pretty tall order."

On the verge of tears, she pressed herself into the propped-up pillow, squeezed her lips tightly together, and crossed her arms, locking her hands into her armpits. "Well, for your information, nothing is too hard for my God. I'm trusting Him to take care of everything, and I know He will!"

"If you are counting on God to provide you with a job, you may be out of work for a long time," the man countered with a smile that held no hostility. "You'd be much better off going to an employment agency. At least they'd know where the jobs are."

"God will provide. He always does," she responded with a positive air, willing herself to remain calm and trying to maintain her dignity. Mildred moved up close to the bed, carefully eyeing her patient. "I'm not sure this conversation is good for you."

Keene leaped to his feet. "I–I'm so sorry. I never meant to upset her. I'll come back tomorrow when she's feeling better. I know this day has been hard on her, and she needs rest."

"I won't be here tomorrow. I'm going home as soon as the doctor releases me." Jane stared at the man, amazed he had taken the time and effort to come to the hospital so soon after their accident. He didn't need to check on her, yet he had. He could have simply let his insurance company take care of the details and not been bothered. From the look of his beautifully tailored suit, starched white shirt, and designer tie, he was probably some highly paid executive. However, unfortunately, he lacked the best thing in life. A relationship with the Lord Jesus Christ. Some things money simply could not buy. "Besides, I'm sure you have better things to do with your time than check up on me."

He leaned against the bed, took her hand, and cradled it in his. "Oh, but I wanted to check on you. I'm afraid you're going to be hearing from me a lot for the next few weeks, until you're fully recovered."

"That's not—"

He gave her hand a gentle squeeze. "Oh, but it is necessary. I may not believe in God, but I believe in doing the right thing. Making sure you are all right, your hospital and doctor bills are paid, and your car is either repaired or replaced are going to be the number one priority on my agenda until things are back to normal for you." He gave her a smile that resonated with warmth and concern. "Now, tell me, is there anything I can do to help you?"

Jane stared at him. *Is this guy for real?*

"Just tell me, and I'll do it gladly."

She continued to eye him suspiciously. Although it appeared money was not a problem for him, it was nonetheless a generous offer.

"I don't want you worrying about anything but getting your head and that leg well," he said, and from the sympathy she could read in his eyes, he surely meant what he said. "You must let me do something to help you. Just name it."

She forced a small smile. "Well, if you hear about any job openings, you might let me know."

He paused thoughtfully. "What sort of skills do you have?"

She gave a slight shrug, wincing at the pain in her leg. "I—I really don't have any skills. The only place I've ever worked is Big Bob's Discount House. I started there my senior year of high school, stocking new merchandise, and I've been there ever since, nearly twelve years now."

He gave her a slight frown. "Did you take typing or any business courses in high school?"

"I'm not sure if I took typing or it took me." She chuckled. "I made terrible grades. That typing teacher was cranky and so demanding I cringed every time she looked at me. Even now, all these years later, just the thought of that pretentious woman makes me shudder. I've often thought maybe if I'd had a different teacher, I might have been a better typist. Who knows?"

Keene rubbed his chin as if in deep thought then strode to the window. Jane watched, waiting for him to make some comment, like her dad had done so many times, telling her she should have knuckled down, learned to type, and forgotten about the arrogant teacher. But he didn't. After a few minutes, he turned slowly and, keeping his piercing brown-eyed gaze on her, stepped forward. "I think I may have an answer for you."

two

Jane stared at him, trying to shake the cobwebs loose from her fuzzy brain. *What answer can he possibly provide to my employment dilemma, other than suggest filing for unemployment benefits? As if I haven't already thought of that!*

He moved closer to the bed, so near that without any effort at all she could reach out and touch him if she had a mind to. "When you feel like it, I'd like you to come work for me. Until you can find another job," he added hastily.

If she had felt like laughing, she would have. "Doing what?"

He studied her face, looking at her as if he were seeing her for the first time and perhaps already regretting his blurted job offer. "It's kind of hard to explain."

I thought it was too good to be true.

"I guess you don't know who I am."

She leveled a serious gaze at his handsome face. "You said your name was. . ." *Did he tell me? I can't remember.*

"I'd say that's about enough. I don't want you tiring my patient." Mildred nodded toward him in drill sergeant fashion, moving from her place by the door to stand at the foot of the bed, her arms crossed firmly over her ample chest. She gave the man a stern-nurse look.

"I'm okay, Mildred," Jane answered, curiosity about his answer to her question getting the better of her clouded judgment.

He hesitated, but when the woman continued to stand her ground, he continued. "I need someone to stuff envelopes for mailings, do some filing—general office stuff, answer the phone, run errands, and take things to the post office, that sort of thing. Nothing complicated. I'm sure you could do it, and I wouldn't pressure you. You should be able to drive soon, since it's your left leg."

"I'm not the world's best typist."

He laughed out loud. "I gathered that. I don't need you to break any speed records on the keyboard." He hesitated, and she wondered if he was afraid to ask his next question for fear of her answer. "You do know how to work a computer, don't you?"

She gave him a smile. "Yes, I'm pretty good on the computer, just not a good typist. One of the men at our church gave me his old computer when he bought a new one, and it has become my hobby. I'm on it, surfing the Net, whenever I can find a spare moment."

He appeared relieved. "Good, because I just bought a new one with all the bells and whistles. I'm a novice myself, so I'll be absolutely no help to you."

Now that his offer had finally sunk in, she could hardly believe it. "You're actually serious? About me coming to work for you?"

"Absolutely. You need a job and I need an assistant." His warm and friendly smile was welcome. "I'll pay you whatever your former job paid you, and once that leg of yours heals, you can take off whatever time you need to apply for a more suitable occupation."

Aha! The caveat! "I may not find a job right away. Jobs in Providence are pretty scarce right now. You do understand that, don't you?"

His smile continued to be friendly. "Look," he said, taking her hand in his, "I don't expect you to find a job right away.

In fact, I hope you don't." He chuckled mischievously. "You don't know how far behind I am in my filing and myriad other things. But once you have worked for me—if you do a decent job—I'll be able to give you a good recommendation. That should help you find another job."

His offer sounded like God's answer to the prayer she had been sending up to Him since the moment she was placed on layoff status. But what did she know about this man?

"Jane, I just heard about your accident!"

Jane glanced past her guest and Nurse Mildred, smiling as she caught sight of Karen Doyle, her best friend and prayer partner, bounding into the cubicle clutching a small bouquet of baby roses.

"Oh, sweetie! This is just awful!" The pretty blond-haired woman dressed in a pale blue jogging suit hurried to Jane's side. "I've been so worried about you since Pastor Congdon called and told me some man had run his BMW into your little Chevy Aveo. Are you all right? Does your leg hurt very much?"

"I'm going to be fine. The accident broke my ankle," Jane said, gesturing toward it, "and I got this nasty bump on my head, but other than that, I think I'm doing okay."

Karen's eyes widened. "Oh, honey, are they sure you don't have other injuries? I mean, you could have—"

"No, no other injuries," Jane assured her, gesturing toward Keene. "This is the man who caused the accident. He's just offered me a job."

Karen gave him a snarling stare. "You caused the accident?"

He nodded then looked back to Jane and raised his brows. "Do we have a deal?"

She hesitated. How could she resist such an offer? But what if she couldn't perform the work to his satisfaction? Or he turned out to be difficult to work for?

"You're Keene Moray!" Karen's face filled with a pleased look of surprise.

Jane's gaze immediately shifted to the man's face.

"Jane and I have all your CDs!" Karen went on, moving quickly to stand by him. "What are you doing in Providence, of all places?"

Awestruck herself, Jane pulled up to a seated position and stared at the man, her jaw dropping. "You're Keene Moray!" Her hand went to her chest, and her heart pounded wildly. "I can't believe I didn't recognize you."

He brushed past Mildred, nodding. "Yep. Guilty. That's me."

Nurse Mildred tapped him on the shoulder. "I don't care if you're Elvis Presley come back to haunt us. This girl needs her rest, and you two are keeping her from getting it."

Keene gave the nurse an agreeing smile. "You're absolutely right. She's had enough excitement for one day." Then, turning to Jane, he said. "We'll talk later. Just do what the doctor tells you so you can get well."

Karen patted Jane's hand. "I'd better go, too, honey. I'm due at work in half an hour, but I wanted to see how you were doing and bring the flowers by. I know you like baby roses. Call me when you get home." She turned to Keene with a grin, sticking out her hand. "It was so nice to meet you, Mr. Moray. I can't wait to tell the girls at my office I've actually met a star!"

He took her hand and smiled back at her. "It's always nice to meet a fan."

Both he and Jane watched Karen, and then he turned to her, his smile fading. "I'm sorry, Miss Delaney. I truly am. I never meant for this to happen. I meant what I said. I'll do anything to make this up to you."

Although she was furious with him for his carelessness, his sincerity touched her heart, and she found herself mellowing.

Especially now that she knew who he was. "I'm sorry for my outburst, Mr. Moray, but you have no idea how. . ." She paused, gulping at the enormity of the problems she was facing. "Thanks for coming."

"My offer of a job still stands," he said kindly. "But I really need your answer as quickly as possible. Good-bye, Miss Delaney."

Jane nodded and then watched until the curtain closed behind him. Turning to Mildred she asked, "How soon do you think I can leave?"

Before the nurse could answer, the doctor entered, wearing a warm smile. "I've already signed your release papers. You can leave as soon as you're ready."

ào

Keene sat in the hospital lobby, waiting, unable to think of anything except Jane Delaney. Even with that nasty bump on her head and her dark hair pulled back in one of those ponytail things, he could tell she was beautiful. One look at those wounded blue eyes, and he knew he had to do whatever he could to right the wrongs he had caused. She looked so vulnerable lying there on that bed, her head bandaged, her leg broken. He had wanted to sweep her up in his arms and take care of her, tell her everything was going to be okay. Good thing he'd had a chance to speak to that doctor as he'd left her room. Otherwise, he wouldn't have known she was being released right away.

What a day this had been. He had left the state capitol area, fully intending to drive past the convention center and then return to his condominium to get a little work done. Instead, he had spent the last hour in the hospital emergency room. Not that he minded, because he didn't. The accident *had* been his fault. The least he could do was try to make things up to the poor, unfortunate woman who had been driving the other car.

He snickered audibly as their conversation about her God filtered through his mind. *Too bad she is willing to put her faith in a myth. How can she possibly believe there is a God?* Although his years of training had centered on his voice and his music, he had taken a few scientific courses in college that totally disproved God's existence. Surely, no one with any sense at all could believe in such a fairy tale.

Well, her beliefs were her own. As long as she did not try to force them on him, they would get along fine. Drumming his fingers idly on his knee, he glanced at the big wall clock. How long could it take to check out of the hospital? He had already told the accounting department he would take care of all her bills.

"Could you call a taxi for me, please?"

He turned quickly toward the voice coming from near the reception desk, and there she was, sitting helplessly in a wheelchair, her foot propped up on the footrest. Jane Delaney. The woman whose life he had ruined in one careless second. He rose and hurried to her side. "You don't need a taxi. I'll take you home."

The look she gave him told him that his plans were not her plans. "Thank you, Mr. Moray, but that won't be necessary. I–I know you're a busy man. You've already done enough by paying my bill." Her voice was gentle but firm, leaving him unsure of what to say next.

"But I insist. I'm the one who upset your life."

With a sigh that could only mean exasperation, she gave him a disparaging look. "I've already asked this nice lady to call for a taxi. I don't mean to be rude, and I *am* a great fan of yours, but—"

"You're afraid to ride with a stranger, is that it?"

"I—I guess so."

"I'm completely harmless, I can assure you." He moved a step closer. "Taking you home is the least I can do."

She turned to the woman at the desk, who sat waiting for further direction, the phone still in her hand. "Go ahead, please. Call a taxi. I can't impose on this nice man."

Keene had never taken rejection kindly, in any form. "You're sure you won't change your mind?"

Jane fiddled with her purse's shoulder strap, and he knew she was avoiding his eyes. "I—I'd better take the taxi home."

He stood staring at her, thinking how people crowded around him at the end of his concerts, begging for his autograph. And how he couldn't go anywhere without someone literally hanging on to his coat sleeve, trying to strike up a conversation about one of the arias he'd sung or their favorite CD he'd recorded. However, this woman was different. She was actually trying to avoid being with him, and somehow he found it almost refreshing—challenging. He raised his brows in question. "You are going to accept my offer, aren't you?"

She lifted her big blue eyes to meet his, and once again he noticed how pretty her delicate features were, despite the huge knot on her forehead. Her complexion was flawless, giving those blue eyes a China doll quality.

"Do you really want me to work for you, or are you just being kind?"

"Of course I want you to work for me. I made the offer, didn't I?" He hoped his smile was convincing.

She returned his smile, although it seemed somewhat guarded. "Then, yes, I accept, but only until I'm able to get out of my cast and find another job."

He decided to push once more. "You'll come to work for

me, but you won't accept my offer of a ride home?"

❧

Jane felt a flush of warmth rush to her cheeks, and she couldn't do a thing to stop it. Keene Moray, the man whose voice echoed through her apartment nearly every night, was standing in front of her. The man she'd admired since she had been old enough to buy her own CDs. Most of her friends had laughed at her when she told them her favorite artist was an opera singer instead of a country music vocalist. Even Karen had laughed, but once she had visited Jane's apartment, ridden in her car, and listened to his rich voice and elegant phrasing, she, too, had become hooked on the music of Keene Moray. When he'd recorded his *Love* album, featuring the most romantic songs of all time, both she and Karen bought two copies—one to play and one to save. She had dreamed about attending one of his operas or concerts someday, when she could afford it, seated in the front row, close enough to see his handsome face and watch his expressions. Now here he was—offering her not only a ride home but also a job! A real job! Though only a temporary one.

"I'd like to, but—"

"But you never accept rides from strangers, is that it? Even if they've demolished your car and put you in the hospital with a broken leg and a banged-up head?"

"I—I have to admit I do feel a bit strange about it." She felt her blush intensify. What a fool he must think her. And she certainly didn't want him, the famous Keene Moray, to see the dingy, low-income apartment she lived in. "I—I hope you understand. I don't mean to offend you."

He gave her a compassionate grin that made her feel a bit better. "Okay. Let's strike a deal. If you refuse to let me take you home, at least let me pay for your taxi. Remember, it's because of me and my carelessness that you're not able to drive your car."

He was right about that. His carelessness had put her in this quandary. She was glad he acknowledged that fact. "Okay. I guess."

"Your taxi is here," the receptionist said, gesturing toward the double glass doors.

Jane allowed Mr. Moray and the orderly to help her through the doors, out of the wheelchair, and into the waiting taxi. She watched from the backseat as he spoke a few words to the driver and paid the man with a bill that would do far more than cover her trip across town. Waving at him through the window, she mouthed the words "thank you" and then settled back for her ride home, resting her injured leg on the cab's leather seat. Good thing she'd worn a dress that day, instead of her good slacks or jeans; otherwise, they would have had to split them up the sides, and she certainly couldn't afford to buy a new pair.

When the car moved forward, she suddenly realized she had not even given him her phone number, and she had no idea how to call him. How could she go to work for him if neither one knew how to reach the other? Then she remembered he had taken care of her hospital bill. Perhaps he had written down the information from that.

When they reached the exit from the parking lot, the driver pulled to one side and waited, holding his microphone and relaying the address she had given him to the dispatcher. Assuming he was waiting for a response, she was not surprised when he continued to wait before pulling out onto the street. After a few minutes, he nodded into the rearview mirror and pulled out into the line of traffic. Curious, she turned and glanced out the rear window.

There, not more than twenty feet behind them, sat a dark blue BMW convertible, bearing a dent in its fender and hood, a broken headlamp, and a few scratches to its bumper, with Keene Moray at the wheel. He was following them! Surely, he would be turning off soon. He wouldn't follow them all the way to her home, would he? *Please, Lord. No! Even though I am thankful to have a roof over my head, I do not want him seeing where I live!*

Stealing a glance every so often, she kept close watch on the BMW, hoping the next time she looked it would be gone. It didn't happen. Each time the taxi changed lanes or made a turn, the BMW did, too.

"This it?" The driver pulled the taxi up in front of one of Providence's low-cost housing development apartment buildings.

With a final backward glance, she pointed to the group of apartments at the far end of the development. "There, just beyond the playground equipment, where the lady is standing beside the wheelchair."

He pulled up to the curb and waited while the friend Karen had called from the hospital helped her into the chair. After making sure the door was closed, the driver nodded and drove off, leaving her sitting at the curb with her friend when the BMW pulled up beside her.

She watched, her heart pounding, as the handsome singer flashed her a smile that set her head reeling. He was even better looking in person than he was on the TV shows she had seen. "I–I didn't know you were going to follow us," she stammered, feeling utterly ridiculous.

"Of course I followed you. That man was a stranger. You'd never ridden with him before." The glint in his eye made her blush again. "I wanted to make sure you arrived home safely."

"This is my friend and neighbor, Ethel Cawkins," she told him, gesturing toward the frail, white-haired woman standing beside her. "My friend called her before I left the hospital. She was kind enough to loan me her wheelchair now that she no longer needs it."

He gave the woman a pleasant nod. "How nice of you, Mrs. Cawkins." Then, turning back to Jane and grasping the chair's handles, he said, "I'll help you to your door."

Panic set in. If he left that BMW convertible parked there with its top down for even five minutes, someone would no doubt remove the CD player and strip off the hubcaps, maybe even take more items. She had seen it happen before. "No, you can't!"

However, he was already pushing her toward the door with Mrs. Cawkins trailing behind. "Oh, but I must. A true gentleman always sees a lady to her door. I'm afraid you're stuck with me."

"But. . ."

Ignoring her protest, he rolled her right up to the door. "Through here?"

She stood her ground. "Wait! You don't know what happens to fancy cars like yours. The hoodlums who live here can trash a car quicker than you can imagine. I can't let that happen to you."

"But we have things to talk about." He grabbed the door handle. "I need to know when you can come to work for me, a phone number where I can reach you, that sort of thing. And I want to make sure your car is taken care of properly and in a timely fashion. Until you have it back, or one to replace it, I am going to be your chauffeur! Take you wherever you want to go."

The Keene Moray? *Her* chauffeur? The thought actually made her want to giggle. Moving quickly, she yanked the handle on the right wheel, spinning the chair around so it blocked the doorway. "You can't do that!"

"Oh, but I want to. Or, if you prefer, I'll rent you a car."

The latter offer had more appeal. She would not allow him to be her chauffeur, no matter how much he insisted.

"My, but you're a stubborn little thing. I can see by your expression you would rather be independent. Well, I cannot say that I blame you, although I would be happy to chauffeur you anywhere, at any time. Since you will not accept my offer of being your chauffeur, I will phone my car dealer and have him deliver a nice rental car to you. Is that acceptable?"

This had to be the most thoughtful man she had ever met or ever hoped to meet. She did need a car to get around, and what he said was true. Through his carelessness, he had taken away her only means of transportation. "Yes, a rental car would be very nice, but you really don't—"

"I want to. I cannot bear the idea of you being without transportation. Besides, you'll need a car to get to my office." That grin again, and she nearly wilted.

"This is far enough, Mr. Moray. Mrs. Cawkins will help me get into my apartment. Thank you for making sure I got home okay."

He raised a brow. "Are you sure? I'll be happy to see you safely inside."

She shook her head. "No, this is fine."

With a slight shrug, he reached into his pocket and pulled out a small notepad. "If you insist." He scribbled something on it and handed it to her. "This is my address and phone number. I don't want to pressure you, but I could really use your help. Give me a call when you feel up to going to work."

"I'm sure I'll feel up to it by next Monday. The doctor said I can begin walking on this leg in a few days, though I may need crutches or a walker for a while. Would Monday work for you?"

"Monday will be fine."

He eyed the wheelchair.

She nodded toward her neighbor. "Mrs. Cawkins has been kind enough to loan me her walker, too. I'm sure I'll be able to manage without help."

"Good." He seemed satisfied with her answer and backed away a step. "If you have any trouble, you give me a call. Why don't you report for work about nine?"

Work. How good that word sounds. God works in mysterious ways. If it hadn't been for the accident, with the scarcity of jobs for unskilled workers, I might have been without a job for weeks. What would Mom and I have done then? The few hundred dollars I've managed to save for a rainy day sure wouldn't have gone far.

She gave him a broad smile. "Nine on Monday."

"I can count on that?"

She laughed. "Yes."

They bid one another a friendly good-bye, and then Jane and Mrs. Cawkins moved into the dimly lit hallway. Instead of heading toward her apartment, which happened to be on the ground floor, she positioned her chair in a shadowy area off to one side of the door. A chill ran through her when the BMW moved out of sight. *I am actually going to be working for Keene Moray!* Quickly, she bowed her head, promising God she would do her best to be a testimony for Him to this man who didn't believe in Him.

❧

The following Monday, with fear and trepidation and Karen at her side, Jane parked the rental car in the visitor parking lot of prestigious Kennewick Place and pulled out the walker Mrs. Cawkins had loaned her. She had tried to use a set of crutches another tenant offered, but they made her feel wobbly and hurt her armpits. She felt much more secure using the walker. She hobbled her way to the elegant entryway, questioning her sanity. *Whatever made me accept his generous offer?*

Despite its beautiful exterior, the elaborate building gave her the creeps. She had no business being in a place like this—for any reason—and she felt like an intruder. Kennewick Place reeked of opulence and wealth. With Karen's help, she opened the door and moved inside. A brass-framed roster on the wall listed the names of the occupants, and she began to scan it for the name *Keene Moray*.

"Wow, this is some place," Karen said, surveying their beautiful surroundings. "I know you were afraid to come here alone your first time, before you had a chance to check things out, but are you sure he won't be mad that I came with you?"

"I hope not." Finally locating his name, she pressed the button beside it and they waited. After what seemed an eternity, his magnificent baritone voice boomed out at her from the speaker.

She identified herself, waited until the buzzer sounded, allowing the door's lock to be released, then manipulated the walker carefully down the hallway and headed for his condo. She'd been leery about coming to a near stranger's condo, but after he explained he was using it not only for a home but also as an office while he was in Providence, she'd felt much better about it.

"Look, Karen. It's plain and simple," she said, hoping to convince herself even more than her friend. "I need a job and he needs an assistant. This is nothing more than a business arrangement. One of my friends, a secretary, has worked for an attorney who has his business office in his home for a long time, and it's worked out very well for both of them."

Karen gave her hand an assuring pat. "I'm sure things will be just fine."

Jane's heart raced at the idea of facing Keene Moray again. She had been so out of it the last time she saw him. Probably even giddy since the doctor had given her something to mask the pain in both her leg and head. Now it was even hard to remember the conversation they'd had. Had she made sense? She doubted it. Having never taken pain medication before, there was no telling how it had affected her. She didn't even want to think about it.

She closed her eyes and held her breath as each step took her closer to his condominium. What was she doing here anyway? She hoped this wasn't a mistake.

"Well, you made it! Come in."

Sucking in her fear, she looked up into Keene's smiling face when he met her in the hallway. "Good. . .good morning, Mr. Moray," she managed to mumble, nearly losing her balance manipulating the walker through the wide opening. "I asked Karen to come with me. I hope you don't mind."

"Not at all. Hello again, Karen." Turning his attention back to Jane, he said, "I hope that leg hasn't caused you too much pain." He gently took her arm and walked slowly beside her a few yards down the hall to an open door.

Causing me much pain? It has been nearly impossible to get comfortable. "It hasn't been too bad."

"How's the head doing?"

It's really been hurting. "Not too bad. The doctor is going to take the stitches out Wednesday."

"And the rental car they brought you? Did it meet with your approval?"

There was no reason for her to avoid the truth here. "My approval? Oh, yes! It's the nicest car I've ever driven. Much nicer than my Aveo, and way bigger."

He laughed good-naturedly, stepping out of her way once they were inside. "Good, I'm glad you like it."

Karen grabbed a magazine from a stack on the coffee table and seated herself on the sofa. "I'll sit here while you two talk."

Jane nodded. She was greatful her friend had come with her.

Keene's condominium astounded her. The living room was large and filled with sunlight from the long stretch of sliding glass doors that opened onto a huge balcony overflowing with potted flowers and palms. Both the walls and the sculptured carpets were off-white, with the furniture upholstered in shades of green and burgundy, and highlighted with touches of royal blue and rose. A grand piano stood in the far corner, an oversized vase on it filled with fresh flowers. It reminded her of a room from a movie set or an architectural magazine. Far more impressive than any she had ever been in before.

"My place in New York City is a bit nicer, but this one will do. I'll only be here for a few months. A friend of mine owns this condo, but he's spending a year in Europe, so he's been kind enough to loan it to me." He clasped his hands together and raised his brows. "May I get you something to drink? Water, soft drink?"

Jane shook her head, feeling like a country bumpkin for the way she allowed herself to stare at both him and the room. She couldn't help it. It was all so grand. "Nothing, thank you."

He motioned toward a wide hallway. "Do you need to rest before I show you where you'll be working? I'm sure it's not easy getting around in that walker with your leg in a cast."

"Oh, no. I'm fine, but. . ." Although she was eager to see her working quarters, she paused, wanting to give him another chance to change his mind. The idea of her, a nobody, working for a famous opera star was ludicrous. "You were very kind to offer me this job, Mr. Moray, but if you'd like to back out—I'll understand. I'm sure in time I can find another job."

He carefully nudged her on, his touch nearly melting her. "I won't hear of it! You need a job, and I need an assistant. I'm sure we'll have a pleasant working relationship."

"It's okay. You don't have to help me. I can make it on my own. In fact, in a few days I hope to completely rid myself of this walker." She tried to escape his grasp, but he wouldn't allow it.

"Just take your time. We're in no hurry."

"Remember, I don't have any office experience," she reminded him.

He stopped and stared at her, his demeanor light and teasing. "Office experience? How much office experience does it require to file things in alphabetical order?" He gave her a mischievous grin. "Didn't you learn that little song when you were in kindergarten? You know the one I mean. A, B, C, D, E, F, G, and so on? The one that ends, 'Now I've sung my ABCs. Tell me what you think of me.' "

Even though it was a silly children's song, Keene Moray had just sung those few words for her—personally, an audience of one! The idea made her head swim.

"Well, did you?"

"Yes," she finally admitted, "only I have another version I like better."

"Oh? Sing it for me." He moved to stand in front of her and waited.

She nearly fainted at the thought. *Me sing? For the great Keene Moray? Unthinkable!* "No! No, I couldn't do that."

He gave her arm a slight squeeze, sending icy chills through her body.

"Come on. I insist. You do sing, don't you?"

"Yes, a little."

He tipped his head, eyeing her. "I'll bet you sing at church."

"Yes."

"In the choir?"

She nodded.

"Then you must sing for me."

He waited expectantly, and she knew he was not going to give up until she had sung the little alphabet song for him. She swallowed a lump that had suddenly arisen in her throat and sent up a quick prayer. *I promised You, God, I would be a testimony to this man. Make me brave enough to sing it for him.*

"Jane. Sing. I'm waiting. Come on. I sang mine for you."

"Promise you won't laugh at me?"

"I promise," he said, sobering and crossing his heart with his index finger.

She began, hoping she had started in the right key. "A, B, C, D, E, F, G. Jesus died for you and me. H, I, J, K, L, M, N. Jesus died for sinful men, a-men! O, P, Q, R, S, T, U. I believe God's Word is true. U, V, W. God has promised you. X, Y, Z. A home e—ter—nal—ly."

The ridiculing look she expected to see on his face did not happen. Instead, the faintest of smiles appeared as Keene seemed to be assessing her words. "That's pretty cute. Great way to learn the alphabet. Did you make it up?"

She could not help but smile back. Every child who had ever attended her church had learned that little song. And they had sung it at every youth camp she ever attended. "No, I didn't, but I wish I could take credit for it. Everything it says is true."

"You have a nice voice," he said, leading the way down the hall and pushing open the door that led to his office.

She couldn't be sure if his compliment was sincere or merely polite, but she was grateful for it anyway. *Thank You, Lord!*

"How long have you been singing in your church choir?"

She followed him into the room, trying to keep her mind on his question instead of the magnificent office that surrounded her. She had nearly forgotten about Karen waiting in the living room. "Since my first year of high school, but I've belonged to the junior choir since fifth grade."

He motioned her toward an upholstered chair in front of a wide cherrywood desk and then seated himself in a chair next to it. "Ever done any solos?"

She sat down in the comfortable chair and swiveled it to face him, lifting her foot and resting it on the edge of a heavy metal wastebasket. "Yes, a number of them, although I'm not that good. They only call on me when they're desperate or someone is out sick."

He gave her an accusing grin. "I doubt that. I think you are just being modest. From the little bit I just heard, I'll bet you're very good."

"Is. . .is this where I'll be working?" she asked. This time it was she who wanted to change the subject. Discussing singing with Keene Moray was like racing a rowboat against a cruise ship, and it made her ill at ease.

"Yes." He turned and pointed to a pile of boxes lined up along the wall. "Those are what I need filed. Most of it is sheet music. Some are contracts. The rest is a conglomeration of letters, clippings, research, and I can't even remember what else. I had all that stuff shipped here to Providence, hoping to find someone like you who could go through it, sort it all out, and set up a filing system for me." His finger pointed toward a row of boxes piled on top of one another. "Those boxes are all empty filing boxes. I figure once they are filled, it will be easy to ship them to my office in New York. And those boxes are filled with office supplies," he said, pointing to a few boxes at the far end. "Mostly file folders, labels, envelopes, staplers, that sort of thing. If I missed anything you need, we'll get it."

He pointed to a big box on the credenza behind the desk. "That's fan mail that needs to be sorted and answered. I guess I could write out a simple letter, have it duplicated, and send it to everyone, like many of my artist friends do, but I like to respond to my fan mail with a personal note to each person who has taken the time to write me. From the looks of things piled around here, you can tell I have gotten way behind. I'll need you to take care of those for me, too." He gestured again toward the stack of mail. "Maybe you could start with those fan letters. That way you wouldn't have to walk around very much. I don't want you overdoing it."

She stared at the boxes, taking them in one by one. "What if I have questions? Will you be here to answer them?"

He threw back his head with a raucous laugh. "Oh, yes. I will be here, but you'll probably wish I wasn't! I'll be learning and practicing a new opera for next year's season, and I'm afraid at times I get very loud." He sent her a toothy grin. "Perhaps I should provide earplugs for you."

Earplugs? To block out that fabulous baritone voice? Never! "I won't need earplugs, Mr. Moray. I'll love hearing you practice."

A deep frown creased his brow, and she feared she had said something wrong.

"Look, if you and I are going to be working together, you'll have to quit calling me Mr. Moray. Call me Keene. That is my name, you know. My real name, I might add. Not a stage name."

Her flattened palm went to her chest and her eyes widened in awe. "I can't—"

"Oh, yes, you can. You must call me Keene. I insist." His smile returned. "And I can assure you I get pretty testy when I don't get my way." He pointed to her walking cast again. "By the way, when did the doctor say you could get rid of that thing?"

"Hopefully in five to six weeks. I'm ready to start work if you'll show me what to do. But first I'd better tell Karen she can go on home."

He rose, rubbing his hands together briskly. "Fine! Let's get at it."

"You're sure you don't need me to stay?" Karen asked when Jane hobbled into the living room. "Can you really trust that guy?"

Jane smiled. "Yes, I'm sure I can. Go on now, and I'll call you tonight."

"Good thing we each drove our own car," Karen added with a nod toward the hallway. "Call if you need me."

Jane assured her she would. Once the door closed behind her friend, she headed back down the hall, confident she was perfectly safe with her new boss.

For the next three hours, they worked side by side with Keene opening the boxes containing all the items he had mentioned, going over the contents in detail, and telling her how he wanted them sorted. At noon, he called for sandwiches to be delivered by a nearby deli. Although the sandwiches were delicious, Jane found it hard to swallow. Just being in the presence of this famous man made her stomach quiver and her hands shake with delight. His kindness toward her was amazing. He stopped her from doing anything that would hurt her leg or cause her discomfort.

They worked until three when Keene suggested they call it a day. When the door closed behind her, Jane leaned against the foyer wall and breathed a deep sigh. She had gotten through her first day of working for Keene Moray, and it hadn't been half bad. It fact, it had been extremely pleasant. Now if she could just come down off cloud nine and get home without tripping over something.

ès

As soon as Keene heard the door close, he moved into his office and phoned the garage where they had towed Jane's car. "You are going to repair it as good as new, aren't you?" he asked Biff Hogan, the job manager.

"Depends on how much your insurance company wants us to do," the man said. "That's a pretty light little car. That BMW of yours banged it up real good."

"Perhaps it'd be better to replace it. From what the owner said, I assume it's around six months old, and I doubt she's put very many miles on it."

"You're right about that. She's chalked up less than four thousand miles." There was a pause on the other end. "I doubt your insurance company will replace it. They rarely do, but the costs to repair it back to its original state are going to be pretty hefty."

Keene pondered his words carefully. Somehow it didn't seem right to repair something that had been nearly new before he damaged it. "I'll be right over. I want to take a look at it myself before you do anything, okay?"

"Sure. You're the boss."

All the way to the garage, Keene's thoughts were on Jane and the misery and inconvenience he had caused her, and how sweet she had been about the whole thing. He thought about the time the two of them had spent together that day, going through the boxes, setting up the filing system, and eating lunch together. Although he regretted meeting her by running into her car and causing her injuries, it seemed fate had brought her to him. She was exactly the kind of person he'd hoped to find to fill the temporary assistant position during the time he would be in Providence. Even with that cast on her leg slowing her down, he knew she'd do the job efficiently, and it would be nice to have someone with her pleasant disposition around the condo, not to mention the strain it would remove by having someone to field his incoming calls.

He smiled to himself. Especially the calls from the many women he had dated while in New York and even those who often called from Paris—beautiful, well-educated women who knew and appreciated good music. He loved having a beautiful woman on his arm when he attended the many social functions required of him as a performer, but there wasn't one among them he would ever want to marry. No. When, and if, he ever married, it would not be to some debutante who had more interest in maintaining her figure and keeping her artificial nails in perfect condition than in being a loving mate to her husband and bearing his children. It would be to a real woman. One who would put him first, and if God allowed—

If God allowed? He laughed out loud. *God? There is no God. I merely quoted a figure of speech! Like talking about the tooth fairy or Mother Nature.*

He pulled into a parking stall in front of the automotive shop and turned off the ignition, for the first time realizing he had been humming to himself. A tune he couldn't place at first. Then it hit him, and he began to sing aloud. "A, B, C, D, E, F, G. Jesus died for you and me." An audible huff escaped his lips. *Jesus? Jesus never actually lived. He was a fable—a myth, just like God! Nothing but a silly myth!*

Biff walked toward him and stuck out his hand as Keene entered the building. "Looks like you're gonna have to have that little Chevy Aveo repaired instead of replacing it. Your insurance company won't go for the whole ball of wax," the man shouted over the loud noise of grinders and sanders. "Come on into my office!"

Keene shook the man's hand and followed him into the office, seating himself across from Biff's beat-up old desk. He looked the man directly in the eye. "Tell me, Biff. If this were your daughter's car and you could either fix it or replace it, without any insurance company being involved, and you were the one responsible for wrecking it, what would you do?"

The man remained silent for a minute, then grinned. "Well, as the owner of this body shop, I'd say I'd fix it up."

"And as a father?"

Biff Hogan rubbed his fingers across his cheek, roughing up the small amount of stubble that had grown there since his morning shave. "If I were the father, I guess I'd have to say replace it. Wouldn't seem fair to pawn off a repaired car to replace one that had been nearly new and without a scratch before I banged it up."

"I agree wholeheartedly. Haul that Aveo over to the General Motors dealer and tell him to get in touch with me with a price for a new one—exactly like it, using this one as a trade-in. Okay? It's the only fair thing to do."

❧

Two days later, at the end of their workday, Keene led Jane through the Kennewick Place lobby to the parking lot, where a red Aveo was parked.

"My car!" She rushed over to it and then realized something was different. Peering in the window, she noted both the dashboard and the upholstery were a different color than hers. Backing away quickly, she felt a flush of embarrassment rush to her cheeks. "I—I guess I made a mistake, but it looked like my car."

Without a word but smiling broadly, Keene reached into

his pocket and pulled out a key. "It is your car, Jane. A brand-new one. Here, try this key in the lock."

Puzzled, she stared at him. "But your insurance agent said my old car could be fixed up to look like new."

"*Look* like new—that's the operative word, but your car would always bear signs of being wrecked. If not on the surface, at least underneath. If you ever tried to sell it or trade it in, it would depreciate the value. I couldn't let that happen. I caused the wreck. I had to replace it with one that had not been wrecked. I–I hope you like it. I told the dealer I wanted it to be as close in appearance as possible." He stepped forward and rested a hand on the car's top. "If it isn't right, or you'd rather have another color, I told—"

"No! It's perfect just as it is, but I never expected you to buy me a new car!"

"I only paid the difference between what my insurance paid and the selling price of a new one. I'm just glad you like it. Now," he said, still holding on to the key, "go on and enjoy your evening. I'll see you in the morning. Don't worry about the rental car. They'll be picking it up this evening."

After taking the key and opening the door, Jane smiled at him with tears in her eyes. "I've never met anyone like you, Keene."

He chuckled. "Let's just say you bring out the best in me." He rested his palms on the top of the car after she climbed inside and rolled down the window. "I've never met anyone like you either."

His words made her tingle all over. She hoped they were a compliment. At least, she was going to take them that way. She handed him the key to the rental car, said another sincere thank-you, then a quick good-bye, rolled up the window, and turned the key in the ignition. Taking in the fresh smell of her new car, she backed out of the parking space and headed for the exit. If she could have her pick of men, it would be a man like Keene Moray.

The next few weeks flew by as Jane worked at a whirlwind pace, trying to put things in order the way Keene wanted them. At times she felt frustrated when her walking cast kept her from moving as quickly as she would like, making certain projects tedious and laborious, but he never seemed to mind the delay and was more than patient with her.

That patience was tested the day before the doctor was to remove her cast. In her excitement, she accidentally knocked a file box off a chair. It contained the sheet music Keene was using to rehearse for the next season, and every piece ended in a heap in the middle of the floor, mixed up and scattered. Knowing how important the order of his music was to Keene, she began to cry as she knelt and tried to gather them up, barely able to read the titles and page numbers through her tears.

When he entered the room and realized what had happened, he waved his arms and spouted a few profanities, which only made her feel worse. Unable to deal with her self-recrimination, much less his fury, she collapsed into a heap beside the mess she'd made, weeping her heart out, her cast sticking out awkwardly in front of her. She had wanted so badly to please him.

He crossed the room slowly, coming to stand beside her, wringing his hands as if he had no idea what to do or say. Finally, he knelt on one knee and wrapped his arm about her shoulders. "I'm. . .I'm sorry, Jane. For a moment there, I lost my head. I'm not mad at you. Seeing everything on the floor like this upset me because I knew how much work you'd put into filing that box full of sheet music."

She lifted her eyes to his, tears cascading down her face.

"I—I thought you cursed because you. . .you were mad at me! Maybe now that I'm getting rid of this cast, it's time for me to get out of your way and look for another job."

"No! Like I said, I'm not mad at you! Things happen. I have done far worse than spilling a box of mere paper, and I wasn't even wearing a cast. Look what I did to you and your car. I know how hard you've worked to get everything in that box in order!" He stroked her hair gently then wiped a thumb across her damp cheek, clearing away a tear. Tilting her face up to his, he gazed at her, his deep brown eyes filled with regret. "I apologize for my language. I am sure you are not used to hearing words like those. And don't you even talk about finding another job. I would like you to stay on right here until I am ready to leave Rhode Island. I—I don't know what I'd do without you."

She had a hard time finding her voice with him so close she could feel his breath on her cheek. She wanted to say something profound, something that would convince him of his lack of reverence for God, but the words wouldn't come. *Lord, help me! I promised to tell Keene about You and Your saving grace, and I'm making such a mess of things!*

Her boss gave her a gentle smile. "For your sake, I'll try to have better control over my mouth in the future, but old habits are hard to break. You may have to remind me occasionally. Give me a swift kick. But I really want you to stay. Promise me you will?"

"I—I'd like to stay, if you're sure you want me," she murmured, dazzled by his touch and enjoying being near him.

"I said I did, didn't I?" He gave her a warm smile. After searching the room for a larger empty box, he helped her put the fallen items into it. "You can refile these when you have time. Why don't you quit and go on home? This will wait until tomorrow," he said once everything had been picked up from the floor. "Besides, I have a dinner engagement, so I'll be leaving early myself."

Her heart sank. Even though she was nothing more than a temporary employee, it hurt to think of another woman sitting beside him, smiling at him over some exotic candlelight dinner at a swanky restaurant. She had never considered the fact that he may have a girlfriend in Providence. Of course he would! This was Keene Moray, the singing idol of thousands of women throughout the world. Somehow, the thought filled her with jealousy, a feeling completely foreign to her. Realizing the fallacy of her thoughts, she snickered.

"What?" He pulled away from her and rose. "What's so funny?"

Embarrassed and unable to think of one reasonable excuse to explain her silly actions, she simply gave him a blank stare. "Ah. . .it was nothing. Your. . .your statement about having dinner reminded me of something, that's all."

He tilted his head and lifted a brow. "Oh, you have a hot dinner date, too?"

His choice of the word *hot* distressed her almost as much as the word *too*. Her face probably showed it. She had never used the word *hot* in that context, let alone had a *hot* dinner date of her own. "No, Mr. Mor. . .Keene, I don't have a dinner date. I'm planning on reading a book tonight."

"Hey, I'm sorry." He placed a placating hand on her wrist. "I never meant to offend you, Jane. *Hot* was just a figure of speech. You know—like exciting—no, not exciting. Interesting. Special."

Keene Moray actually looked—embarrassed? If she hadn't been offended by his use of words, she would have enjoyed it.

"I think I know what you mean," she offered, amused to see

someone so famous put on the defensive for something he had said, and to her, of all people. A nobody.

"Hey, since you're from around here, maybe you can help me decide where to take Camellia for dinner tonight. It's her birthday, and I want it to be a surprise."

"I—I really don't know much about Providence's fancy restaurants, but I have driven past The Green Goddess a number of times. It looks pretty fancy."

Knotting his hands into fists, he pressed them into his lower back and arched, stretching first one way and then the other. "I guess I should get more exercise. I sit at the piano far more than I should." He gave her a lopsided grin. "I'm going to be an old man before my time if I don't change my ways."

"You could join the YMCA." The words slipped out before she realized what a ridiculous suggestion she had made. Why would he join the Y when he could afford to belong to the fanciest health club in town?

She watched a slow smile creep across his mouth. "Not a bad idea, except for one thing. There are great workout facilities right here in this building, and I don't even take advantage of those."

She felt just plain dumb. "I—I hadn't realized."

"I didn't know it either until two days ago." He grinned again. "Too bad you have that cast on your leg, or I'd invite you to try out one of their treadmills."

"I—I've never used a treadmill," she admitted dolefully.

"I hate them. My idea of exercise is a fast game of tennis. Now that's a real workout."

"I've never played tennis either." She had worked weekends one summer at the local country club, waiting tables for those who did know how to play tennis or at least walked around the clubhouse carrying their expensive rackets and wearing cute little tennis outfits.

"I was kidding about the fast part. I'm not very good myself. Always too busy to take the time to improve my game." He tossed an imaginary ball into the air, swinging at it with an imaginary tennis racket, and then chuckled. "See, I didn't even get it across the net."

She loved his sense of humor. Surprisingly, nothing about him seemed pretentious or conceited. She giggled, covering her mouth. "Maybe your racket has a hole in it."

He pretended to be lifting it up, observing it carefully as his hands twisted back and forth. "You know, you may be right. Maybe I'm a better server than I thought."

"You. . .you don't look like you need to exercise. You look, umm, fit to me." *More stupid words. I'll bet his Camellia wouldn't say something that stupid. She would probably ooh and ahh over him, stroking his biceps and saying how strong he looks.*

He smiled again. "Aw, thanks."

"Well, I'd better get out of here so you can get ready for your date." She stood and picked up her walker, setting it directly in front of her before swinging the strap of her bag over her shoulder. "I'll see myself out."

She started for the door, but the phone rang. Out of habit from answering it the past few weeks, she reached for it without even looking his way. "Keene Moray's residence. This is Jane. How may I help you?"

There was a pause on the other end of the line, then a sneeze. "I need to speak with Keene." Another sneeze. "Tell him this is Camellia."

He took the phone, and after a few "uh-huhs" and an "I'm sorry," he said, "Perhaps another time, when you're feeling better." Before hanging up, he stared at the phone for a few moments then turned to Jane.

three

"Camellia had to cancel our plans for this evening. How about having dinner with me at that swanky restaurant you told me about? The one with all the cars in the parking lot. To celebrate the official removal of your cast tomorrow."

Jane's knees threatened to bend of their own accord. If she had not been hanging on to the desk, they probably would have. "No. . .no, I'm sorry. I–I can't."

"Why not? You have to eat supper. We can order a take-out dinner for your mother, if that's what's stopping you."

"It's not that! Mom is able to get herself something to eat when I can't make it home."

"Then why?"

Her gaze immediately went to her simple tank dress and chiffon cover-up blouse. "I'm. . .I'm not. . ."

He must have caught her concern. "Okay, we'll go somewhere else. Maybe have a steak at one of Providence's famous steakhouses. Would that be better?"

Seeing that he wasn't going to give up easily, she glanced at her watch. "I have choir practice at seven thirty."

His smile was devastating. "No problem. It's nearly five. If we head out now, you should have time to do both." He stepped toward her and placed his hand on her shoulder.

Ripples of joy coursed through her at his touch. To think that he—Keene Moray—would invite her—Jane Delaney—to have dinner with him was nothing short of incredible.

"Come on, Jane. Say yes. I get tired of eating alone. You'll be doing me a big favor."

"Well. . .I guess. . ."

"Is that a yes?"

She nodded. "I–I guess. If you're sure. . ."

His hand went from her shoulder to cup her chin as he lifted her face to his. "I'm sure. Now put that walker in gear, and let's go have a steak."

ta

A few minutes past seven thirty, when Jane arrived at the church, choir practice had already begun. She slipped into the seat next to Karen as quietly as she could, opened the folder lying on her chair, and pulled out a piece of sheet music, frantically searching for a word or phrase that would give her a hint as to which page they were on.

Karen leaned toward her and whispered with a grin, "You're late. Page four, at the bottom."

"Thanks." Although Jane loved singing in the choir and learning new music with which to praise her Lord, she found her mind wandering back to the wonderful time she'd had at the restaurant with Keene. He was gorgeous, with such a striking presence it had seemed all eyes turned toward him when they entered. Something about him and his appearance commanded attention. He exuded confidence and an assurance about himself that few men did. She found herself still in awe of him. Apparently, others did, too. Several people came to their table seeking his autograph.

When the last note had been sung, choir director Ben Kennard smiled and held up a folder. "Okay, folks, you've got that one down pat. We'll be doing it a week from Sunday. We'll go over it one more time next week."

Karen slipped the music back into her folder and leaned toward Jane. "You're never late. What happened?"

"You'll never believe it. I'll tell you later."

"Take out the music for *Down from the Cross*," Ben told them, holding up a fairly good-sized book. "We're coming along quite nicely with this. I am proud of all of you, but remember, we not only have to know *how* to sing the music, we have to sing it with feeling. Why?" He paused for effect, his eyes scanning the faces of the 150 members of Randle-wood Community Choir. "Because we're singing it for our Lord. Yes, there will be those in the audience each of the eight nights we perform *Down from the Cross* as a citywide Easter pageant whom we hope and pray will be touched by what we sing, but touching those hearts is God's job. If we give Him the best we can, He will do the rest."

"I–I have a hard time singing this cantata without crying," Emily Stokes, one of the altos, said as she opened her folder. "The words really speak to my heart."

"Me, too," Gene Reynolds, the lead bass singer, boomed out. "God had to have inspired the man who wrote this music."

Winnie Martin touched her handkerchief to her eyes. "Just thinking how Jesus suffered and died for us—well, I praise Him for. . .for. . ." Halting, she began to weep.

"It's okay, Winnie. I think this cantata touches each of us in a special way." Ben bowed his head and said softly, "Lord, each of us comes to You this night with our own special load of baggage. We ask You to take it from us, lift it from our backs. Cleanse our minds of all thoughts except those of You. May we praise You with each word we sing, that Your name may be glorified. We ask these things in Jesus' name."

"Amen," the entire group said in unison.

Ben motioned toward an empty seat in the baritone section. "As most of you know, Jim Carter has been having some physical problems lately, and he's asked for our prayers. I'm. . .

I'm sorry to have to tell you, but they have determined he has throat cancer. He has an appointment with a specialist tomorrow to see how best to proceed. We need to continue to pray for him. The prognosis does not look good."

Winnie stood to her feet, her eyes round with concern. "But he always sings the part of Jesus! What if—"

"If he can't sing," Sarah Miles interrupted, tears evident through her thick glasses, "will. . .will we have to cancel the cantata?"

Everyone waited for Ben's answer.

Ben frowned, gripping the edges of his music stand. "At this point, Sarah, I would have to say yes, that's a distinct possibility, but it's in God's hands. Easter is only eight weeks away. It would be very difficult for someone else to step in and learn the music at this late date. I know you are all disappointed to hear it, but *Down from the Cross* may have to be canceled. The church board will be making the final decision within the next day or so. Until then, I guess we'll carry on as usual."

"But—" Sarah began.

"Let's not discuss this any further tonight. We need to get on with our practice. The best thing we can do at this point is pray for a miracle for Jim when he goes to the specialist tomorrow. We all know God is able to perform miracles."

Karen leaned toward Jane. "We simply can't do the cantata without Jim."

Jane gave her a weak smile. The news had upset her as much as everyone else. Jim Carter, a professional performer who traveled most of the year with a Southern gospel quartet, had sung the lead baritone part in their cantatas for as long as she could remember. Although she had heard him many times over the years, his rich voice still sent chills down her spine, even in rehearsals. "I know. We'd better pray hard."

After another hour of practice, Ben dismissed the group.

"Jane, can you stay?" he asked as she moved out of the choir loft. "I'd like to go over your solos again."

"Sure, Ben. I've been working on them at home, and I could really use your help. But if *Down from the Cross* has to be canceled—"

"It hasn't been canceled—yet." He motioned her toward the microphone. "I'm wondering about the part on page fifty, Jane. Even if we have to cancel the cantata, I still want you to sing this part on Easter Sunday at all three morning services."

"You do?"

"Yes, I do." He adjusted the microphone for her and then stepped aside. "Remember, you're playing the part of Jesus' mother. Before you begin to sing, think how Mary would feel. Put yourself in her place. Try to experience the same emotions she would have felt. Elation when she witnessed the miracles He performed. Sorrow when He was mistreated and falsely accused. An overwhelming grief as He was led to the cross."

Ben's words tore at Jane's heart, and she found herself unable to speak.

"For these few minutes, you *are* Mary, the mother of Jesus. Be her. Respond the way she would respond. Weep as she would weep. Cry out the way she cried out. Forget about the audience. Do this for Him, Jane. Your Lord. Your God. The One who took your sins upon Himself and died on the cross for you. Think of His pain, His agony as He hung there on the cross, as Mary would have thought of it. Take on her personality. Her demeanor. And yes—her burden. If you cry—so be it! If you have to stop and compose yourself before you can go on—so be it! Become Mary, Jane! Forget who you are, and be who God wants you to be at that moment: Mary—the mother of Jesus—and sing it from the depths of your heart."

Without picking up her book, Jane lifted the walker and moved one step closer to the microphone. She knew her part by heart. She had memorized it weeks ago. With a quick prayer to God, she nodded toward the pianist and began to sing. It was as if it were not her voice she heard but the voice of Mary, singing the way Mary would have sung it, and her heart rejoiced. *This is for You, God; I'm singing it for You!*

"That's it!" Ben rushed to her side when she finished. "That's exactly what I wanted. Oh, Jane, that is the best you have ever done it. Surely God has touched both your voice and your heart."

Tears of joy flowed down Jane's cheeks later when she thought over the evening's events while hobbling her way across the nearly empty parking lot to her car. "Thank You, Lord, for giving us Ben Kennard as a choir director. Surely, You sent him to us. Help me to sing the part of Mary as I did tonight, so souls in the audience may see their need of a Savior and turn to You. And please, God, be with Jim Carter. He needs your touch."

❧

"Well, did you make it to choir practice on time last night?" Keene asked when Jane entered his office at ten the next morning, fresh from a trip to the doctor's office.

Jane smiled at him, holding out her leg, minus the cast. "Not exactly on time, but close."

"You finally got that thing off. Congratulations!" He knelt and wrapped his hand around her slim ankle. "How does it feel?"

"Nude!" She laughed, shocked at the word she had used to describe the weird sensation of having her ankle exposed to air once again. Hoping to make him forget her ridiculous remark, she hurriedly added, "It seems a bit strange to walk on it, but it feels marvelous—absolutely marvelous—to finally be rid of that cast."

"I'm sure it does. I'm amazed you've done so well with it."

He followed her down the hall to his office. "So how did choir practice go?"

"Wonderfully well." She wanted to tell him all about the things Ben had said to her, about becoming Mary when she sang the part, and how, because of his words and guidance, she had sung better than she'd ever sung before, but she knew he wouldn't understand and kept it to herself. "We've been working on our Easter cantata for weeks now. It's beautiful."

"Easter cantata, eh?"

"Yes, it's called *Down from the Cross.* The writer had to have been truly inspired by God."

He waited until she was settled in the desk chair where she planned to work on his fan mail and then seated himself in the chair opposite her, resting his elbows on the desktop. "I don't know about that. Think of all the wonderful works of music that haven't been inspired by God. Many of them have survived the test of time quite nicely."

She could not hold back a grin. Chalk one up for God! Keene trapped himself by that admittance and did not even realize it. "Haven't been inspired by God? Does that mean you acknowledge His existence?"

He reared back in the chair with a hearty laugh. "Oh, you thought you caught me, didn't you? That is not what I meant at all. I meant, *you* thought they had been inspired by God. Not me!"

Somehow, singing the part of Mary in the strong way she had the night before gave her a new boldness. "What about Handel's *Messiah*? Was it not inspired by God? Do you think that man came up with it all by himself? We've all heard the story of how that miraculous piece of music came to be written. Handel himself declared it had been inspired by God."

"I think you and I could argue this point until doomsday and never come to a resolution." He stretched his arms first one way and then the other. "Too heavy a topic for this early in the morning. Besides, I've got practicing to do, and you've got mail to work on." With that, he stood and headed for the door. "I'll call for pizza for lunch. That okay with you?"

She nodded, forcing a smile, fully aware he was dodging the issue. How could he be so blind?

Thursday and Friday went along routinely, with Keene practicing in his room and Jane working in the office. Occasionally, she would open the door a crack, listening to the voice she loved to hear, amazed at the way the two of them had been brought together. However, in her heart she felt like she was failing God. She had promised to be a witness to Keene. Now, all these weeks later, he'd come no closer to believing in God's reality than the day they first met. "Lord," she prayed in a whisper, "this is the most wonderful man I've ever met. He has been kind, considerate, and gentle with me, yet each time Your name is mentioned, it's like a wall goes up between us. I don't know how to reach him. I need Your help, Your guidance. I don't know what to do. Help me, please."

ə

Everyone sat in the chairs, waiting. The choir director was late to choir practice.

"Maybe we'd better go on without him," one of the men suggested impatiently.

"Maybe he's had an accident," one of the female choir members said with concern.

All eyes turned as Ben entered the side door and moved up to his place in front of them. From the downcast look on his face, everyone could see something was troubling him. A hush fell over the choir, creating an awkward silence in the big sanctuary.

"I'm—" He stopped and cleared his throat noisily. "I'm afraid I have bad news. After a number of tests and a biopsy, the doctor has determined Jim does indeed have throat cancer and cannot sing with us. He'll be seeing another specialist tomorrow to decide how best to proceed."

Jane and the others turned toward one another, audibly voicing their sorrow and concern that something this terrible could happen to such a wonderful, dedicated man. One who used all his talents for his Lord.

Ben raised a hand to silence them. "The church board called an emergency meeting. They've asked me to tell you we are definitely canceling the Easter pageant."

Women began to cry, and men shook their heads, many of them blinking back tears as well.

"Without Jim Carter to play the part of Jesus—" He didn't have to finish his sentence. Everyone knew, without Jim, the pageant would not happen.

"We're all disappointed, Ben," one of the tenors volunteered, standing to his feet. "I'm sure we'll all be holding Jim up in prayer."

Everyone nodded in agreement.

"I'll tell him. I know he's counting on your prayers." Ben swallowed hard and then continued. "I honestly thought this year would be our best year yet, with more souls saved than ever. *Down from the Cross* has such a message to it. Like all of you, I'm. . .I'm sorry and disappointed, but without Jim, we have no alternative. Believe me, Jim is more disappointed than any of us. He'd really looked forward to this year's Easter pageant."

Josh Steward rose slowly. "I really praise the Lord for Jim. Some of you who have been here as long as I have will remember the first time we talked about doing an Easter pageant here at Randlewood Community Church. A number of us—including me—were very much opposed to even having an Easter pageant, especially with an earthly man playing and singing the part of Jesus. Somehow it seemed irreverent. A group of us on the church board attended the pageant another church was performing, just to get a firsthand look at the performance and the audience reaction. I sure wasn't prepared for what we saw that night, and I don't think most of the other board members were either."

J.T. Fortner rose, nodding. "I went that night, and like Josh, I was one of those who did not want our church to do an Easter pageant. Although I knew the man hanging on the cross was only another man, a sinner just like me, I can't tell you the emotions that rushed through me as I sat in that audience. I'd never attended anything like it, and for the first time—seeing an actual scene of what it must have been like for my Jesus to suffer and bleed. . ." He paused, covering his face with his hands. "I—I think that's when, for the first time, I really came to grips with what He has done for me. I remember turning to the chairman of our board and telling him I'd changed my mind. I wanted our church to do an Easter pageant."

Wiping his eyes with his handkerchief, Elmer Bones stood, too. "That night will be embedded in my memory forever. Oh, I know some folks think it's wrong to portray Christ's life and death in a dramatic way, with mere mortals acting out the scenes, but since our church started having annual Easter and Christmas pageants, I dare say we've seen hundreds of lost souls flock to the front when our pastor gave an altar call. My. . .my. . ." He stopped, weeping openly, and gestured toward a lovely white-haired lady in the alto section. "My. . .my dear wife was one of them, praise God." He sniffled and rubbed a tear from his cheek with his thumb before going on.

"I have to wonder how many of those people would have accepted Christ as their Savior if they hadn't been in that audience that particular night. I, for one, am glad our church board had the foresight to vote unanimously to do these pageants. I have seen God's hand at work not only on those who attend the pageants, but in the lives of us choir members. I say—if there is any way possible—we keep doing them."

A rousing "Amen" sounded from all persons sitting in the choir loft.

"Isn't there someone else who could sing Jim's part?" one of the sopranos asked, blotting her eyes with her hanky.

"The board thought of that, but we only have about eight weeks left before Easter. For someone to step in at this late date, even if we could find a suitable substitute, would be nearly impossible. They'd not only have to learn the singing part but the stage part, too, with all its movements and locations. No, with the little amount of time we have left, that would never work, and we cannot risk doing a shoddy performance. Not for our Lord. He deserves only our best."

"You're right. I'm sorry I mentioned it." The soprano lowered her head and sat down.

Ben brightened and smiled. "We still have this Sunday's specials to practice." He turned to the group of six sitting on a long pew in front of the choir. "On your feet, gang." The six immediately moved into position, picking up their guitars and strapping them on while the pianist took her place.

Karen leaned toward Jane and whispered, "How could God

allow something like this to happen?"

Though she had not voiced it, Jane wondered the same thing. The news about Jim's illness hit her hard. For the fourth year in a row, she had been asked to sing the part of Mary. Though she had nearly turned Ben down the first year he asked her, the other members of the choir had encouraged her to do it, many saying her lovely alto voice would be perfect for the part. Even now, she could remember how terrified she had been at the idea of singing the solos before the many thousands of people who came to hear their Easter cantata each year. Nearly every one of the tickets for the eight performances were given out weeks ahead of Easter. Their church never charged those who attended, but you had to have an advance ticket to get in. Many nights, people were waiting in line as early as six o'clock, hoping folks wouldn't show up and they'd be given their seats at the last minute.

There had been talk of moving the performance to another place, like the city's convention center, but the board had always voted it down. They feared moving it to a location outside the church would make the cantata lose some of its warmth and atmosphere. Besides, over the years, the behind-the-scenes production committee had learned to handle things quite well in their familiar surroundings.

As their practice ended, Ben clapped his hands loudly. "Attention, everyone. Since we won't be needing the music for *Down from the Cross* any longer, leave your books on your chair, and I'll gather them up and take them to my office later." He offered a sympathetic smile. "Maybe next year Jim will be back, and we'll be able to sing it."

Jane rose slowly, giving the precious book one last look. Though she had bought her own personal copy so she could practice at home, she never brought it with her for fear she would leave it at the church. She had also bought the accompaniment tape. She allowed her fingers to trail lovingly across its cover of deep royal blue. Below the title was an empty wooden cross with a long diagonal blast of sunlight reflecting from behind it, shedding light on the otherwise dark cover. The symbolism touched her heart deeply. *Christ came to a dark world to take on my sin and die a tragic death for me! But His life didn't end there. He arose. Praise You, Father.*

"I'm just sick about this." Karen Doyle placed her book on the seat with a shake of her head.

"So am I, Karen, but God is sovereign and promises to work all things for good to those who are called according to His purpose." Jane carefully placed her book on the seat, slung her purse strap over her shoulder, and moved toward the aisle.

Karen followed. "A lot of people are going to be disappointed. I've really been talking it up at the office where I work. I'd planned to get at least twenty tickets to pass out to my coworkers, and I think most of them would've come. I've been trying to tell them about their need of God in their lives, but it's so hard. I'd so hoped *Down from the Cross* would touch their hearts and make them want to accept God."

Jane allowed a sigh to escape as she trudged toward the door, her heart heavy with disappointment. "I was hoping my boss would come, too."

Karen's face brightened. "You really think he would have?"

Pausing, Jane turned to her friend. "Maybe. I haven't asked him yet, but I'd planned to."

Karen harrumphed. "You needn't worry about that now."

"Yeah, I know."

The two friends hugged and went their separate ways, promising to have lunch together soon.

ta.

"What's wrong, Jane? You have been quiet all morning. Aren't you feeling well?"

Jane had not been able to get the church's Easter pageant off her mind since choir practice the night before. She almost hated to tell Keene about it, sure he would gloat and remind her that God wasn't real, that if He had been real, He never would have let their main soloist become ill.

"Jane? I asked if you weren't feeling well. Did you hear me?"

She looked up at him, blinking back tears. She hated getting emotional on him, but that's the way she was, and she couldn't do anything about it. This had really upset her. Jim Carter was a Christian brother and she felt for him and his family in this time of crisis. She felt bad for all the choir members who had worked so hard learning *Down from the Cross*, and all those who were helping with costumes, makeup, scenery, tickets, and the hundreds of other things that supported a production of this size and magnitude.

Keene circled his arm about her shoulders and looked down into her face. "What is it? You can tell me, you know that, don't you?"

"It. . .it's nothing you'd be interested in."

Using his free hand, he pulled a pristine white handkerchief from his pocket and blotted her tears. "I've never seen you so upset." A tiny smile turned up the corners of his mouth. "Except when I crashed my BMW into your little car."

"I'm just disappointed, that's all."

He frowned, and in his eyes she could see a genuine concern. "Oh? At someone or something?"

She gave him a wistful look. "The man who always sings the part of Jesus in our Easter pageant has throat cancer, and his prognosis doesn't look good. Without him, we've had to call it off, and I was so looking forward to singing the part of Mary. We're all praying for him, but even if he has surgery, there's no way he'll be able to sing by Easter. Maybe never!"

Keene pondered her comment for a moment then asked, "Isn't there someone else who could sing his part?"

Jane checked the coffeemaker and, finding Keene had already made their morning coffee, poured each of them a cup. "No, not the way he sings it. He has sung the lead part in our cantatas for as long as I can remember. Besides having a great voice, he really puts his heart into it."

"Thanks." He took the cup from her hand and stared into the rich brown liquid. "Well, learning an entirely new score in such a short time would be quite difficult, but learning the stage moves and timing that quickly, too, would be nearly impossible. It'd be difficult for me to do it, and I'm a pro."

"Enough of this kind of talk." She picked up her own cup, forcing a smile. "I've got work that needs to be done today, and you've got practicing to do. See you at noon."

He gave her a mock salute with his free hand. "Yes, ma'am."

The phone was ringing when she entered the office. Another one of Keene's many girlfriends, this one calling from London, wanting to know why he had not returned her calls.

"I'm sorry. I've given him all your messages," she explained to the impatient woman. "However, I can tell you he is in the midst of learning new music for his next season and is quite busy." She took the woman's name and number again. *How many times has that woman called?*

At noon, she gave him the call slip, along with several others—most of them from women who had called before. "You're a popular man," she said, smiling at him over a carton of sweet and sour chicken. "It seems most of the calls I take for you are from women."

He grinned. "What can I say? I admit I enjoy the company of beautiful women."

She eyed him with a frown. "But you've never married?"

"With my schedule and all my traveling?"

It is none of my business, but I am going to ask you anyway. "Don't you want a wife and children?"

He stared off into space thoughtfully, and she knew he was weighing his answer before stating it. "Sure, I'd like to have a wife and family. However, with my lifestyle, it just would not work. Besides, there's an even greater problem than my schedule and traveling that keeps me from getting married."

"Oh? Dare I ask what it is?" She looked at him cautiously, wishing she could retract her words. He may have a physical problem he would prefer not to discuss with her. She would never want to embarrass him—or herself! And what business was it of hers anyway?

Quickly turning his attention toward her with a mischievous smile, he confessed, "I haven't found the right woman."

Her mouth gaped. That was not the answer she had expected. "You've got to be kidding! With all the women who call you? Keene! Surely you're not serious!"

His expression sobered. "Oh, but I am serious. As much as I value the many female friendships I've made over the years, and the times I've enjoyed the pleasure of a beautiful woman's company for an evening, I can honestly say I haven't found a single one I'd want to marry and call my wife." He dipped his head shyly. "That sounds a bit pompous, doesn't it?"

She considered his remark. "No, I don't think it makes you sound pompous. If you haven't found that one perfect love— the one God. . ." She stopped short and bit her lip.

"The one God intended for me?" He gave her a playful wink.

"Yes, that's what I was going to say," she answered demurely.

He set his carton of lemon chicken on the table and reached across, cupping her hand in his. "Is that what you're waiting for, Jane? A perfect man?"

She felt her eyes widen. "I'm not looking for a perfect man. I'm looking for the man God has intended for me. No earthly man is perfect." She took a deep breath. *I have to say this right, so he'll understand.* "Keene, God has a plan for each of us. His perfect plan. If we love Him and want to serve Him, He'll guide us to the one with whom He would have us spend our life."

He gave her hand a slight squeeze. "Does that mean—out there somewhere—the man of your dreams is looking for you?"

She offered a nervous snicker. "I hope so, but only if God intends that I marry. Maybe, in His perfect plan, I'll remain single all my life."

Keene reared his head back with a hearty laugh. "No way! You are beautiful, intelligent, and one of the most caring, considerate women I have ever met. Some man is going to come along and snatch you up. Take my word for it."

His complimentary words caught her off guard, and she found herself speechless.

"Actually," he said slowly, sizing her up, "those qualities are exactly what I'd like to have in a wife."

Although she couldn't see her own face, she knew it must be as red as a radish.

"Tell me, Jane. What qualities would you like your husband to have?"

As his thumb stroked her hand, she actually felt goose bumps rise on her arms. She hoped that he wouldn't notice. "Ah. . .I. . ."

"Surely, you've thought about that. Don't be shy. Tell me."

Oh, Lord—give me the words. "First and foremost, he'd have to love God as much as I do."

Keene leaned toward her with a tender smile. "Knowing you, I expected that to be your first priority."

Thank You, God. "Well. . .he'd have to be kind, caring, and considerate."

"You haven't said handsome or rich," he prodded with a teasing smile.

"Neither of those things is important to me," she confessed honestly. "I want him to be beautiful on the inside, of course. I don't care about handsome. Nor do I care about rich. I know the man God would have me marry would want to provide adequately for his family. We'd be a team."

"What about children?"

That subject always made her smile. She longed to be a mother someday. "Oh, yes. He'd want children. I cannot imagine God ever pairing me with a man who didn't. Not with the love for children He's placed in my heart. I'd like to have at least four or five."

Keene blinked hard then stared at her. "Four or five children? Really?"

She nodded. "At least. Don't you want children?"

He released her hand and leaned back in the chair, locking his fingers over his chest. "If I didn't have to travel. I could not bear the idea of going off and leaving a family behind. Kids need their dad around."

"It would be difficult. I know I couldn't do it."

He rose quickly. "I've got an appointment in half an hour. I'd better be heading out." He reached for his empty cartons, but she got to them first.

"You go on. I'll take care of this."

He wadded up his paper napkin and stuffed it into one of

the empty cartons before making sure his wallet was in his back pocket and heading toward the door. "Been good visiting with you. I enjoy our little talks."

She gave him a sheepish smile. He'd never know how much she enjoyed them. "Me, too."

Jane worked at the desk, taking care of routine things like making out checks for Keene's bills, answering the many phone calls that came in from all over the world, getting out the mailings he'd prepared for those on his select fan list, and dozens of other chores. But something niggled at her mind all afternoon.

At four o'clock, she called her pastor.

❧

Jane glanced nervously at the clock on the wall in Pastor Congdon's office. Nearly eight o'clock. Without warning, a side door opened and Kevin Blair, a longtime member of Randlewood Community Church, crooked his finger at her. "You can come in, Jane. We're ready for you now."

As Jane followed Kevin into the large room adjoining the pastor's office, she glanced around the big table at the many familiar faces of those who served on the church board.

"Gentlemen, I received an interesting phone call from Jane this afternoon. I have invited her here this evening to tell you, in person, what she told me. I think you'll be interested."

Jane's heart sank into her shoes. She rarely spoke to a group, other than to the women of her Bible study, and even then she shook while she talked. She waited until Pastor Congdon had seated himself before drawing a deep breath and asking the Lord to help her state her purpose clearly and concisely.

"I–I. . ." *Please, God. Calm me down.* "I'm as upset as anyone about our Easter pageant being canceled. Those of us who sing in the choir and have had the opportunity to practice *Down from the Cross* were excited about its message and how both the words and music could touch hearts. It's. . .it's the most powerful testimony to God's mercy and grace that we've ever heard."

She paused, glancing around the table at each person. *God, give them open minds, please.* "I have an idea—a way that will allow us to go ahead with our plans to present the Easter program."

"Without Jim Carter?" one of the older men interjected quickly, his beady eyes staring at her over funny little half-glasses perched low on his nose.

"Hear her out," Pastor Congdon said quickly.

Jane gave him a grateful smile then continued. "I won't go into detail, other than to say that through a series of circumstances that I feel came from the hand of God, I now work for Keene Moray. Some of you may recognize that name."

Some nodded their heads, acknowledging that they did indeed know who he was, while others gave her a blank stare or turned to the person seated next to them in bewilderment.

"Isn't he that famous opera singer?" one of them finally asked.

She nodded. *Don't let them close their minds before they hear me out, God.* "Yes, Keene is quite famous, highly respected in the music world, and very much in demand."

"What's that got to do with our problem?" The man with the little glasses leaned back in his chair, crossing his arms over his chest.

"Like I said, I work for Keene. He is making his home in Providence for the next few months, learning and rehearsing the new opera he will be performing next year. We've. . .we've become good friends."

Pastor Congdon cleared his throat. "Go on. Tell them your idea, Jane."

Her heart raced. If she didn't feel God's guidance in this, she would run out of the room and never look back. "I—I don't know if Mr. Moray would have any interest in what I am about to propose, or if it's even possible with his contract, but I'd like the board's permission to ask Keene to sing Jim Carter's part—the part of Jesus—in *Down from the Cross*."

One of the younger men leaped to his feet and glared at her. "Do you have any idea what it would cost to hire someone like him? I know the church wouldn't be able to afford it!"

"I'm sure he has a contract of some sort that requires union fees. We sure couldn't afford to pay him that kind of money," another added.

Jane chose her words carefully. "I—I was hoping he'd figure out a way to do it for a minimal fee, maybe even gratis."

"Why would he do that? He's never even been to our church, has he?" another asked.

Pastor Congdon stood and leaned forward. "Gentlemen, if I may, I'd like to add something to what Jane has said."

All eyes turned his way.

"When Jane called me, I was skeptical about this idea just like you are. But the more she talked, and the more I listened, I realized this could be the answer to all our prayers—prayers that, in some way, God would make it possible to provide this community with the truth of His Word through our Easter presentation."

He paused and rested his palms on the conference table. "This man may not even consider Jane's idea, but then again, maybe he will. She feels it is worth a try to ask him. I agree with her."

"But is he saved? Does he know the Lord?" a man seated

next to the pastor asked.

Jane felt she should answer his question since she was the only one personally acquainted with Keene. "No, he is not saved, though I have been witnessing to him nearly every day. At times he seems open, and I'm praying he'll confess his sins and ask God's forgiveness before he leaves Rhode Island. He's a wonderful man and a gentleman. You'd all like him."

"I've always questioned anyone playing the part of Jesus, even Jim Carter, but an unsaved man? I'm not sure that would be wise," another man offered, concern written on his face.

"I understand what you're saying, Milton," Pastor Congdon said kindly. "But let's think about this carefully. What is our goal here? Is it not to reach the people in our community with the message of God's Word? Through music and the spoken word? Isn't that the reason we always have an altar call at the end of each performance?"

"But an unsaved man singing the part of our Lord?"

Pastor Congdon rubbed his chin. "Tell me, Milton, do you know for sure that each member of our choir is saved? We have a big choir, some 150 people on any given Sunday. Some folks just like to sing and want an outlet for their talent."

Milton stared at him for a moment before answering. "I hate to admit it, but you may be right."

Pastor Congdon gave the man an appreciative smile. "Let me bring up another point here. We have a fairly large orchestra to back up our choir on Sunday mornings, right?"

Everyone present nodded.

"Have you forgotten we hire about half of those people? They are not even members of our church, but we hire them because they are professionals and we need them. The other half are our own dedicated church members who do it for free because they want to serve God with their talents. Should we fire those whom we hire or think any less of the musicians and their capabilities because they may not claim to be Christians?"

Milton spoke up again. "But hire a man to play the part of Jesus? Shouldn't the man who plays that part be a Christian?"

"That's what we're here to decide," the chairman of the board said, scanning each face. "At this point, we don't even know if Mr. Moray would consider such an invitation should we decide to offer it. He may give us a flat no, and that'll be the end of it." His face took on a gentle smile. "But I personally think Jane's idea has great merit. Think about it. Each year, though we fill our sanctuary for eight straight nights, and we've done everything but get down on our knees and beg the newspapers, radio, and television stations for coverage, we've had very little publicity. And," he went on, "I'm sorry to say, but although many people come forward for salvation or rededication, most of those in our audience are Christians."

Pastor Congdon nodded his head. "He's right. All you have to do is look at the attendance cards we ask everyone to sign."

"What if—" The man's eyes sparkled as he continued. "What if Keene Moray, a famous opera singer, were to sing the lead part in our Easter production? Think of the possibilities to reach people with the gospel, gentlemen. People from all over the state would come to hear him! What would it cost them to attend a performance at the opera? Maybe $60 or $70 a seat? And they would be attending our performance for free! I am not sure we would be able to contain the crowds! Do you think we'd have to beg the media for coverage with him singing the part of Jesus?"

Milton shook his head. "I know you're right—Mr. Moray singing in our church's Easter pageant would be a real drawing card—but could he do it? I mean, portraying Christ would be extremely difficult. Not many men could do it without offending those in our audience. We sure don't want that to happen. I remember the first year we did a cantata that required someone to play the part of Jesus, we had a real uproar from a number of church members."

"That we did," Pastor Congdon said with a slight chuckle. "But after that first night, everyone agreed it worked out well, especially when so many people responded to the invitation. Jim Carter did a masterful job singing, and I don't really remember anyone complaining after that first night."

"But Jim was saved," a member who had been silent up to that point said meekly. "He sang it from his heart."

Jane could no longer keep her silence. "Keene Moray is a professional, just as those musicians we hire for the Sunday morning services are professionals. Granted, he doesn't know Jesus as his Savior, but that man is able to take simple words from a music score and put feelings and emotions into them that would amaze you. I know. I hear him every day. He's not only a singer, he's an actor. A marvelous actor. If he were willing to do it, he could take the music to *Down from the Cross* and make it come alive." *God, help me to make them understand!* "I–I have an audiotape at home of Elvis Presley singing 'Amazing Grace.' I've heard some say he was a Christian, but from his lifestyle, I have my doubts. Yet every time I hear him sing it, it touches my heart. Could not Keene's voice singing the part of Jesus in *Down from the Cross* touch hearts in our audience?"

Pastor Congdon gave Jane a smile of agreement, and she felt herself relax.

"Thank you, Jane," he said, motioning toward the door. "You've given us much to think about. The board and I will discuss this, pray about it, and get back to you. Thank you for coming."

Jane stood to leave and felt compelled to make one last plea. "I—I want to thank you for letting me come here tonight. Please. . .I'd like to leave you with one final thought. Keene is a gentleman with a fine personal reputation, one of which he is very proud. If you decide to allow me to ask him to do this for our church, and if he should accept the invitation, I can assure you he will give the performance of his life. Keene never does anything halfway. He would never do anything to embarrass the church, the board, or me, and especially not himself. Please pray about this and consider it carefully before making your final decision."

She walked out the door with a feeling of euphoria, knowing she had done the best she could. God had answered her prayers and steadied her heart and mind. She had to smile to herself. Getting the church to approve was only the first step. If they agreed, convincing Keene to do it—even if his contract and agent would allow it—might be more difficult. "But," she said aloud with a renewed confidence, "God can do anything!"

❧

The next morning, right at nine o'clock, the phone rang in Keene's office.

four

The caller didn't need to identify himself. Jane recognized Pastor Congdon's cheery "Hello" immediately, and her heart soared.

"We did it, Jane. It took the board another two hours of discussion, but finally they voted unanimously to ask Keene Moray if he would take over Jim's part in *Down from the Cross*. It's up to you now, but I want you to know each man on the board will be praying for you."

She gripped the phone tightly, her heart racing. "Oh, Pastor Congdon, I don't think I slept a wink last night. I just kept praying over and over that God would have His will in this."

"Well, we're only halfway there. He hasn't said yes yet. You can be sure our prayers will be with you while you approach Mr. Moray."

She thanked him for his call then slowly returned the phone to its cradle, all the while smiling and already considering the possibilities if Keene agreed to accept their invitation.

"You're chipper this morning," Keene said, pushing open the door to the office and entering, carrying two glasses of orange juice from the kitchen. He placed her glass on the desk then glanced at the phone. "Who called? I heard the phone ring."

I can't ask him yet. I have to pray about this first. The time has to be just right. "My. . .my pastor."

He shrugged. "Oh, I was hoping Brian, my agent, would call. I need to talk to him today." Pointing toward her glass, he said, "Drink up. You need your vitamin C."

"Thanks, Keene."

She watched him move through the door, amazed at his thoughtfulness. *Lord, even now begin preparing Keene's heart for what I'm about to ask him.*

Fortunately, the work she had planned for the morning was busywork, requiring only repetitive hand motion and very little brainpower or concentration, giving her time to pray for the task she believed God had given her.

For lunch, Keene sent her to a nearby carryout to buy fried chicken dinners. By the time she returned, he had set plates and silverware on the little kitchen table and added ice to their glasses. She quickly fixed a pitcher of iced tea then sat down opposite him, noting he had been unusually quiet most of the morning.

"Something wrong?" she asked, hoping she wasn't prying. She lifted her head after sending up another quick prayer.

He spread a napkin across his lap with a deep sigh. "Not really. Just one of those down days. Nothing you need concern yourself about."

She reached across the table and cupped his hand with hers. Despite the warmth of his skin, cold chills crept up her spine. "Anything I can do?"

He scooted the bucket of chicken toward her. "No, I'm just a bit down. My mom died three years ago today. I wasn't even with her when she died. I was in Japan, singing at some meaningless concert. I've. . .I've never forgiven myself for not coming home when she asked me to."

In all the weeks they'd been together, she'd never seen him like this, and she wanted to do something—anything—to take his pain away. What could she do?

"The doctor had said she wouldn't make it a year. I knew that, yet. . .yet I only made it home to see her twice during all that time. Some son, huh?"

"I'm sure she knew you had obligations," Jane assured him, wanting to free him of some of his guilt.

"Although she was happy for me and my success, she never wanted to be in the limelight," he went on, cupping his free hand over hers and giving it a squeeze.

She watched him blink back tears. Sadness for him filled her heart. "She had every right to be proud of you."

"I remember one time I introduced her and made her stand up, and she nearly fainted." A tender smile played at his lips while he spoke of his mother. "She. . .she left me a letter. I found it in her things when I went home for the funeral."

"I'm sure you'll cherish that letter for the rest of your life."

He removed his hand long enough to wipe at his eyes, then placed it back on hers. "In some ways, she reminded me of you."

She gave him a quizzical stare. "Me? How?"

"She. . .she. . ."

His pause gave her cause for alarm. What could there be about his mother that could have been anything like her?

"She claimed to be a Christian, too."

Awestruck by his words, Jane sat staring at him. "You never told me!"

"Although I loved her with all my heart, those last couple of years I found her to be a little weird. You know, always reading the Bible, attending church, listening to Christian programs on the radio and TV. She used to bug me about going to church with her."

He pulled a handkerchief from his pocket and wiped at his nose. "It happened after she moved into an assisted-living home. Most of the times when I visited her, she'd be her usual old self, bragging about winning at Bingo, planning a trip to Las Vegas to gamble with some of the ladies in the home. But all of a sudden, not long before she died, all she could talk about was God and His love. I could not believe the change. I figured some preacher had come to the home and gotten her all stirred up. However, when I asked her what had happened, she explained that some woman from a nearby church started a weekly Bible study there at the home, and she had been attending. The change in her amazed me. She preached at me like you wouldn't believe. Even on her deathbed when she could barely talk for the pain, all she seemed to have on her mind was God. In that letter she left for me, she kept saying she hoped I'd settle things with God so she would see me in heaven."

"I'm sure it's a great comfort to you to know that she's in heaven with her Savior."

He drew back slightly, his dark eyes locking with hers. "It would be, Jane, if I believed in God. But I don't."

"Your mother believed in Him. Keene, why is it so hard for you to believe He's real?"

He stood, towering over her, his hands on his hips. "You really want to know?"

His aggressive tone frightened her. "Yes, I'd like to know what could make you so bitter toward God."

"My dad walked out on my mom and me when I turned twelve, without so much as telling me good-bye, and I begged God to make him come back home." He dropped to one knee, his eyes level with hers. "You'll never convince me God is real, Jane. I sort of remember a scripture my mom tried to teach me once. Something about an earthly father who wouldn't give his son a stone if he'd asked him for bread. Then it went on to say how much more the heavenly Father wants to give good things to His children if they ask Him. I decided, right then and there, if there really was a God, He would answer my prayers. But nothing happened. I never saw my father again."

"That doesn't mean He isn't real, Keene," she said softly, hoping her words would soothe him. "We can't tell God what to do. We can only ask Him for what we'd like Him to do. I can't pretend to tell you why your father left you or why he stayed away, but I do know God has promised to be a Father to the fatherless."

Keene closed his eyes and blinked hard. "But He let my father walk away from me at a time in my life when I really needed him."

"God would like to be your Father, if you'd let Him."

"Isn't God supposed to be a God of goodness? If He is, why did He let my mother work night and day at a hotel maid's job to keep a roof over our heads? That woman literally worked herself to death!"

She shook her head sadly. If only she had answers. "I don't know."

"If God is real, why did He let that man at your church get throat cancer? And why now? When your church needed him? Answer me that!"

Now, Jane, now. Ask him now, a still small voice seemed to say from within her.

Now, Lord? When he is so angry with You?

Trust Me, child. Trust Me. Now is the time, the voice said.

Jane swallowed the lump that had suddenly risen in her throat and sent up a silent prayer. *If You say so, God.*

"Well, do you have an answer for me? Why would God do such a thing? You've already told me there is no one to sing in that man's place."

Jane rose, her eyes never leaving Keene's. "Because He had a better plan." His stare made her wonder if she had sprouted wings.

"A better plan? Like what?"

Help me, Lord! "He wants you to take Jim Carter's place."

five

"What? Surely you're kidding!" Keene sputtered, nearly choking on his words.

She looked him square in the eye, once again feeling that new confidence she deemed a gift from God just when she needed it. "I've never been more serious."

Keene threw back his head with a laugh that echoed through the condominium. "You want me," he said, ramming one thumb into his chest, "to play the part of Jesus?"

"That's exactly what I'm saying. I've already discussed it with our church board, and they've given me permission to ask you." Though her heart thundered, she was amazed at how calm her voice sounded. "I know you're busy practicing next season's opera, but you're a quick learner. You could do both of them if you set your mind to it. And I'll be here to help you in any way I can."

"Impossible." He turned and strode across the room, leaning his hands on the windowsill and gazing into the blue sky. "Absolutely impossible."

She followed him. "Why? Why is it impossible?"

With a shake of his head, he swung around to face her. "For starters, my agent would never let me do it."

She lifted her chin defiantly. "Oh? I thought your agent worked for you. I didn't realize you worked for him!"

"He does work for me."

"Then tell him you want to do it."

He stared down at her. "I never said I wanted to do it."

She gave him a challenging smile. "But you do, don't you?

Or do you think you're incapable of singing the part?" There, she'd done it. She'd waved her red flag in front of a bull, fully expecting him to charge, but she was prepared for him. After all, God was on her side.

"Of course I could do it. I—"

"It's a pretty difficult role."

He frowned at her, but the smile teasing the corners of his lips told her he was enjoying their repartee. "I've done more difficult, I can assure you."

She put her hands on her hips and took a step closer, jutting out her chin. "Prove it!"

"I'm up to your little game, missy." His hands moved quickly to cup her shoulders. "Look, Jane. Even if I wanted to do it, which I'm not saying I do, I'd have trouble getting this past the union."

"But. . .if you did really want to do it, you could figure out a way, couldn't you?"

He appeared thoughtful. "Maybe. I'd have to work on it."

A chill of excitement rushed through her, and she brightened. "Does that mean you'll try?"

"You realize, if anyone other than you asked me to do this, I'd laugh in their face." He let out a long sigh. "You're not giving me much time. What is it? Seven or eight weeks until Easter?"

"Actually, you'd have seven to prepare. We usually start performing it a week before Easter."

He rested the back of his hand against his forehead. "I hesitate to ask. Is there more than one performance?"

She nodded, beginning to feel quite confident. Hadn't God laid it upon her heart to ask him? "Eight, actually. One each night, including Easter night."

Keene frowned, placing his palms together and templing his fingers as his gaze returned to the window. "That's a pretty demanding schedule."

"I know."

"And you're singing the part of Mary?"

"Yes."

He stood silently for a long time, his vacant stare fixed on the billowy clouds floating aimlessly in the Providence sky. "I owe you, you know," he finally said without looking at her. "Not only for what I did to your car, but for the pain and suffering you went through with your leg."

"I know. I'm counting on that."

"It would be a challenge. I've never sung a part quite like it."

"I have no doubt you could do it."

"I'd have to put my practicing aside and work nearly full-time on learning something totally new."

"You've already told me you're weeks ahead on your new opera." She waited. Hoping. Praying.

"I'd have to work this out with the union."

"I'm sure you'll figure out a way."

He turned to her slowly, his gaze zeroing in on her face. "You think you're pretty smart, don't you?"

His question puzzled her. "Smart? Me? No."

"You just talked me into doing something I wasn't convinced I wanted to do, didn't you?"

His broad smile sent her skyward. She felt like she was floating on one of those billowy clouds. "I talked you into it? Does that mean you'll do it?"

"Only because you asked me. How could I refuse?"

Without thinking, Jane leaped into his arms and kissed his cheek. To her surprise, he held her there, their faces so close she could feel the warmth of his rapid breathing on her cheek.

"Somehow, some way, I'll work it out. You can tell your church board I will be happy to fill in for—what's his name? Jim?"

"Jim Carter," Jane said hurriedly as he continued to hold her in his arms, her feet dangling inches above the thick carpeting.

"Do you realize, Jane, this is the first time I've been asked to fill in for someone? I'm usually the star!"

His voice was teasing, and she knew it.

"This is a pretty humbling experience."

"In my book, you'll always be the star. Thank you, Keene. I know this is going to put a real strain on your time."

"Knowing you, I suppose you prayed about this, right?"

She grinned up at him as he lowered her feet to the floor. "Yes, I did."

He rolled his eyes and shook his head. "And I also suppose you just happen to have a copy of the cantata with you."

"Right here in my backpack."

"You're incorrigible, but you're sweet."

She reached up and touched his cheek with the tip of her fingers. "So are you." *Thank You, God.*

All smiles, he stuck out his hand, palm up. "You might as well give it to me so I can at least see what I've committed myself to."

She grabbed the backpack and quickly located the copy of the cantata and handed it to him. Reaching back in the bag, she pulled out an audiotape. "We'll be using a live orchestra, but this is the practice tape that came with the cantata."

His hand brushed hers as he took the tape from her, and he held on fast, locking his fingers over hers. She thought she was going to explode with joy.

"This should really help. I will start listening to it this afternoon. Right after I clear things up with my agent and the Musician's Union."

"Our next rehearsal is tomorrow night."

He screwed up his face. "That doesn't give me much time, does it?"

"No, but I'm sure you can handle it," she said, meaning it,

thrilled that the wonderful voice of Keene Moray would be singing the part of her Lord. "Oh, Keene, I can't thank you enough."

His finger tapped the tip of her nose, and he smiled into her face. "You're right. You can't thank me enough. Now get to work before I fire you."

She watched him leave the office, closing the door behind him, and then sank into a nearby chair, exhausted but with a prayer of thanks on her lips. "You truly are an awesome God. You've answered my prayer above and beyond anything I could ever imagine, but I have one more request, Lord." She felt a tear slide down her cheek. "Speak to Keene's heart and make him realize his need for You and bring him to Yourself."

❧

Keene closed the door then leaned against its frame. *Whatever possessed me to say yes? I must have been out of my mind to agree to such a thing. The people I will be working with are amateurs. If this Easter thing is not top-notch, it could hurt my career. Not only that, but it will certainly complicate something else going on in my life. Something else important enough to ruin my career.*

His thoughts turned to Jane. *She is the reason I said yes. How could I deny that woman anything when she has asked so little of me? She is the first woman I have met in a long time who did not fall all over herself in my presence. I can be myself with her, totally at ease. I like that. She is the bright spot in my day. I could almost fall for her, if she wasn't so. . .religious!*

Moving slowly to the phone, he dialed his agent's number. "Hello, Brian. You won't believe what I'm about to tell you."

Ten minutes later, after much explaining and arguing with his agent, the two of them reached an agreement. Next, he called the Musician's Union.

❧

Jane waited impatiently for Pastor Congdon to pick up the

phone. Finally, on the fourth ring, he answered.

"God answered our prayer!" she shouted into the receiver. "Keene is going to do it! He's actually going to do it!"

"Jane? This is you, I hope."

She could not contain the joyful laughter bubbling inside her. "Yes, it's me. Sorry I didn't identify myself, but I'm so excited!"

He laughed. "I noticed that."

"He's already called his agent to let him know, and now he's working things out with the Musician's Union. I've given him the music to *Down from the Cross*, and he'll be at our rehearsal tomorrow night!" She finally stopped talking long enough to suck in a deep breath.

"Wow, you work fast! How did you manage to pull it off so quickly?"

"I–I didn't do anything. God did! I just turned it all over to Him and watched things happen. He did it all!"

"Well, I must say, this is good news. I can hardly wait to tell the board and Ben Kennard. I know the entire choir has been praying about this. I'm eager to meet your Mr. Moray."

Jane settled herself into her desk chair and tilted it back, resting her feet on the heavy metal wastebasket. "You'll like him. He's. . .he's. . .oh, I can't think of words to describe him, but he's fantastic!"

"If you say so, I'm sure he is. I had better start calling everyone with the good news. Thanks, Jane, for coming up with this idea and making it work."

"But I—"

He interrupted her. "I know—you didn't do it—God did. But He used you to accomplish it. You were a willing vessel. I'll see you tomorrow night at rehearsal."

Other than stopping for the quick bacon, lettuce, and tomato sandwich Jane made for lunch, Keene didn't come out of his bedroom all day, but while Jane worked, off in the distance she could hear the faint sounds of *Down from the Cross* as the audiotape played. Keene was already at work on the cantata.

The same thing happened the next day. At noon, she had trouble coaxing him to come out long enough to eat a bowl of the broccoli-cheese soup she had prepared especially for him. After drawing a crude map showing the way to the church, she left his office at five with plans for them to meet in the church parking lot at 7:15.

He had already parked his BMW by the time she arrived. A light evening snow had blanketed Providence, causing everything to be slick underfoot. Keene rushed to open her door when she pulled into the empty stall beside him, taking her arm in his as they moved to the church's side entrance. Once inside, they brushed the snow from their clothing and headed for the sanctuary.

While they walked, he scanned the hallways. "This is a beautiful building."

Jane nodded in agreement then took his hand and tugged him along, moving down the long hallway with its many classroom doors on either side.

He stopped long enough to peek into an open classroom. "I wasn't expecting anything like this."

She gave him a grin. "We have indoor plumbing, too." She yelped when she felt a slight pinch on her arm. "And electricity!"

Keene pushed open one of the big double doors when they reached the sanctuary, holding it so they could pass through.

Ben Kennard quickly left his place on the platform and rushed toward them, his hand extended. "Mr. Moray. What a pleasure to meet you. Jane has told us all about you."

Keene gave the man's hand a hearty shake. "Knowing Jane like I do, I'm not sure I want to hear that. We have worked together closely the past few weeks. I'm afraid she knows all my bad habits."

Ben continued to shake his hand. "Believe me, it was all good. You have a real fan in Jane."

"I know."

They walked toward the front of the church with Keene tightly latching on to Jane, cupping her elbow with his hand and sending her a smile that made her toes curl.

She felt a flush rise to her cheeks. "I—I thought maybe it would be best if Keene just listened to our practice tonight, to kind of get a feel for what we've been rehearsing."

"Good idea." Ben reached into his attaché case, pulling out a copy of *Down from the Cross* and handing it to Keene. "You'll want a copy "

Keene held up the one he had brought with him. "Already have one. Jane gave me hers—the accompaniment tape, too." He motioned to an area off the platform, in the center of a front pew. "Why don't I sit there? That way I can see the faces of the people in the choir as they sing. I want to get to know everyone."

After Ben introduced Keene and explained he had graciously consented to take on the lead part and the pageant would go on as planned, everyone took his or her place. They bowed their heads, and Ben thanked God for sending Keene to them by way of Jane, then practice began. Though Jane tried to focus on the choir director, her gaze kept inching off toward her boss. To her surprise, he was mouthing the words without even looking at the book. Then she remembered the many hours, both yesterday and today, she had heard the faint sounds of the audiotape being played while she worked. He had already begun to memorize the music.

At the conclusion of one of the best practices they had ever had, Ben smiled at his group of happy singers. "Okay, gang, listen up! This Saturday is the first of our all-day practices. Again this year, the Women's Ministries group has offered to provide our lunch, so all you will have to bring is yourself. I know it's going to be tough to give up all your Saturdays between now and the time we actually begin our performances, but those of you who have sung in past years know how important these all-day practices are if we are to do our best for the Lord. This is your service to Him. Hopefully, your number one priority. Plan on arriving at nine, and we'll try to have you out of here by four, no later than five." He turned and gestured toward Keene. "It won't be necessary for you to be here all day, Mr. Moray. I'll work with you on a schedule so you'll only need to be here for the time in which you'll be involved."

Keene rose and stepped up onto the platform, facing the choir. "May I say a few words?"

Ben nodded. "Of course."

"First of all, it's nice to be a part of this dedicated group, and I have to say I'm impressed with your singing. I will admit, when Jane first approached me, I thought she was crazy. But"—he smiled in her direction—"when she began to tell me how *Down from the Cross* had been canceled due to Jim's illness, and I saw the look of disappointment in her eyes, I actually found myself wishing I could do something to make her feel better, never realizing the very next day she'd ask me to sing Jim's part." He chuckled. "At first I thought her request might be nothing more than a joke, and I laughed, but then I realized she was dead serious. If anyone other than Jane had asked me to do this, I would have given them a definite no, instantly, without any consideration whatsoever. But Jane? I could never refuse her anything. Not after I turned her life upside down the day I ran a red light and—" He gave her a quick wink. "I'm sure you've all heard the story by now."

Karen gave Jane a playful jab with her elbow.

Keene lowered his head, gazing at the floor for a few seconds before going on. When he looked up at them again, his face was somber. "Jane is a Christian. I am sure most of you are, too. I will not make any pretenses. I am not, but I want you to know I respect your beliefs. I have played many parts in my life as a vocalist, but I have never played the part of Jesus. And although I do not believe in God, I can tell you being asked to play this role is quite humbling, and I am sure it will be the hardest role I have ever taken on. I will give it my very best. That's a promise."

Ben placed his hand on Keene's shoulder. "I'm sure I speak for everyone here, Mr. Moray, when I say we'll all be praying for you. Thank you for your honesty. It's much appreciated."

Turning back to the choir, Keene said, "I'll see all of you at nine on Saturday. Tell those ladies from that women's group to count me in for lunch. I plan to be here all day."

Ben grinned at him. "Jane told us you never do anything halfway. We'll see you Saturday, and welcome aboard!"

It seemed Keene shook hands with each of the choir members before he and Jane were ready to leave, greeting each one cordially and asking their names, telling them how nice it was to meet them. She watched, amazed at his sincere attitude. Then she remembered that this man was not only her friend, her employer, but he was Keene Moray and well used to meeting and greeting fans. She wondered if that smile was really sincere or merely a promotional tool. Either way, the choir members were enjoying it.

"You really didn't have to stay until the last person left, you know." Jane slipped her hand into the crook of Keene's arm and held on tightly as they walked onto the slick parking lot.

"I know, but they're a great bunch of people. I really enjoyed watching them this evening. I think we're going to get along just fine."

The night air felt cold, and a slight breeze had come up, whirling the snow about their feet, giving her an excuse to press in close to him as they walked. "Were you really serious about being there all day Saturday?"

He cupped his warm hand over hers and smiled down at her. "I have to learn an entire cantata. What better way than to follow the book and sing it along with the choir?"

"But you don't have to learn the entire thing, just your part."

"Sorry, but that would never work for me. To do my best I have to know everyone's part, feel the emotion, and see the drama. I cannot just step in and sing. It has to come from here." He took his hand away from hers long enough to point to his heart. "If I'm going to do this, Jane, which I promised you I would, I'll put as much effort into it as I do any of the operas I sing or any of the concerts I perform."

She realized his words should have made her happy, but a thread of disappointment surged through her instead. "Oh, I forgot about your reputation. Who knows? There may be someone from the newspaper or a television station in the audience. You wouldn't want to let them see anything less than a stellar performance."

He stopped walking, grabbed her by the shoulders, and with a deep frown, spun her around to face him. "Look, let's get something straight right now. Yes, you are right about me wanting to give a stellar performance, as you called it. That has been my creed and my goal since the first concert I ever gave—to give my audiences my very best, and I have always done that. Even on nights when I was so sick I could barely hold up my head. If I were singing *Down from the Cross* for an audience of one, I would still give it my very best. That is me, Jane. That is what I do. The performance I give for your church will be the best performance I am capable of giving—regardless of who may be in the audience."

She felt awful. How dare she question his motives, especially after he'd been concerned about her and her church's problems enough to step in and help, taking away from the valuable time he'd set aside to come to Rhode Island and learn a new opera? She lifted her tear-filled gaze to his. "I'm. . .I'm so sorry, Keene. My stupid comment was way out of line. I had no business questioning your motives. Can you forgive me?"

Hoping he understood, she felt a great sense of relief when his intense grasp on her shoulders began to relax. Even in the dimly lit parking lot, she could see her words had hurt him. *God, why do I barge ahead like that? Speak without thinking? I only hope Keene can forgive me. I hope You can forgive me!*

"It's okay," he said softly, still peering into her eyes. "I think I deserved that. I have made some pretty crummy remarks about your God and Christianity. No wonder you doubted me."

"Regardless, I had no right to question your dedication to your profession. I knew—"

He raised his hand to silence her. Then without a word, he gently traced her lips with his fingertip. "Forget about it, okay?"

"But, Keene, you've—"

Suddenly she felt his lips on hers, and she froze, not sure how she should react. Keene Moray was holding her in his arms, kissing her. What should she do?

He backed away slightly then rested his forehead against hers. "I—I couldn't help myself," he murmured as he continued to hold her in his arms. "You looked so kissable."

Jane stood motionless, afraid to breathe or even bat her eyelids.

"You're not mad at me for kissing you, are you?" he asked in a whisper.

"N—no," she finally managed to whimper.

"Would you get mad if I kissed you again?"

Her heart banged against her chest so fiercely she felt sure he would notice. "No."

His lips touched hers again, and she thought she would die of happiness right there in the church parking lot. The moment was wonderful. Spectacular! And she never wanted it to end. Without meaning for them to, her arms wrapped themselves about his neck, and her fingers twined themselves through the slight curls at his nape. Though the pleasant smell of his aftershave made her woozy, she reveled in it.

"Whew," he said, finally releasing her. "I'd better let you get home. It's later than I realized." He reached out his hand.

Confused, Jane stared at it, caught up in the moment, his kisses still fresh on her lips.

"Your keys," he said with an impish grin.

"Oh!" She yanked them from her pocket and watched while he opened her door.

"I've really enjoyed this evening," he told her after she climbed in and rolled her window down.

She struggled to find her voice. "Me, too."

"I'm glad you talked me into this." He gave her a teasing smile. "See you in the morning."

Still having trouble finding words, she simply nodded. Keene gave her a slight wave and headed toward his car.

Jane's fingers rose to her lips as she watched him crawl into the BMW and start its engine. "I think I'm in love!" she nearly shouted, remembering the sweet touch of his lips on hers.

Be careful, My child. Be very careful, a still small voice whispered from deep within her heart.

&

Again, on Friday, Keene spent most of the day in his bedroom, the faint sounds of *Down from the Cross* filtering out from the crack beneath his door. Though neither mentioned their impromptu kisses, their relationship had changed. Jane couldn't exactly put her finger on it, but Keene's smile radiated tenderness, and his voice sounded a little softer. Several times during the day when they would pass in the hall or at lunch, he would slip an arm about her waist and pull her to him.

She even noticed her own response to him had changed. She no longer thought of him as her boss or the famous opera singer, but as. . . What was he to her? She was not quite sure. However, she knew her feelings toward him had changed drastically in the past twenty-four hours. Her every thought now centered on him. Her actions centered on him, too. She wanted to please him in every way. She also noted how much more protective she had become of him. No more did she pass phone calls to him that she thought he might not want. She screened them closely as if she were the FBI. No one could get to him without satisfying her that the call was important. *I am being ridiculous,* she told herself when she hung up from a very heated discussion with a fan who insisted on speaking with Keene. *Who do I think I am anyway? I am certain he got along just fine before I came along!*

The next call came from his agent, Brian Totten. She put the call through immediately and went back to work filing some of the new music he had ordered. But suddenly, even with the door closed to Keene's room, she could hear him shouting at Brian. She couldn't make out the words, but obviously Keene was upset about something.

Five minutes later, he stormed into the office. "I can't believe the gall of that man!"

Jane spun her chair around to face him. "Is. . .is there a problem?"

He towered over her, his hands on his hips, his eyes blazing. "Yes, there's a problem. He is having a fit because I agreed to do this for your church. Not because he's afraid of me taking the time away from my preparation for next year's season, but because he's worried about getting his commission! Can you believe that? With all the money I've paid him over the years!"

She rose and placed a hand on his arm. "I'm sorry, Keene. I never meant to cause trouble between you and Brian."

He shook his head as if trying to shake off his negative feelings, then wrapped his arms about her and pulled her close, nestling his chin in her hair. "You haven't caused any problems, Jane. Brian and I have a round like this a couple of times every year. But what really ticks me off is the trouble the union is giving me."

Her jaw dropped. "Is there a chance you won't be—"

"No, don't even think it. I will work things out with them. One way or another, I'll handle it." He tilted her face up to his, his frown replaced by a smile. "You've changed my life, Jane. I cannot tell you how much I enjoy being around you. You are a breath of fresh air. My life was pretty routine before I met you."

"And I've messed up that routine?"

"Oh, yeah! Big-time, and I'm loving every minute of it."

He gazed into her face, and the tenderness she saw there touched her in a way no man had ever touched her before, sparking an entirely new set of feelings.

"I—I think I could fall in love with you." His words were just a feathery whisper, and she wasn't even sure she had heard them correctly. Surely Keene Moray could not be saying these words to her. Plain little Jane? That is what her father used to call her, and she had felt like plain little Jane all her life.

Be careful, My child. The words coming from the deep recesses of her heart frightened her and made her pull away from him, though she wanted so much to declare her love for him, too. A love she could no longer deny. She took another step backward, pasting on a conciliatory smile. "I—I think I'd better go. I promised Mom I'd be home early, and. . .and. . . I–I have laundry to do."

He reached for her, but she sidestepped him, picking up her purse and car keys from the desk. "See you at nine?"

He let out a deep sigh and pulled his hand away. "Yes, I'll be at the church at nine. I could pick you up."

Shaking her head, she backed out the office door. "Thank you, but I'll drive myself."

 za

Keene waited until the door closed behind her then rammed a fist into the palm of his other hand. *You bonehead! What did you think you were doing? You just told that woman you thought you could fall in love with her! Whatever possessed you to do such a stupid thing? Jane is not like the other women you have known. Any other woman would have been bowing at your feet if you had mentioned the "L" word to them. Now you have probably scared her off.*

After plopping himself down in her desk chair, he tilted it back and linked his fingers behind his head. *What is the matter with me? The* love *word? Since I met Jane, I have even considered the "M" word!*

The phone rang, and he gazed at it for a long time before finally picking up the receiver.

"Hey, buddy, what do you mean, hanging up on me?" the voice asked.

Keene sat up straight, angrily anchoring his elbows on the desktop. "Look, Brian, get this straight! I am only going to tell you one more time. I *am* going to sing in that church's Easter program, and nothing you or the union can say or do is going to stop me."

"But you know the rules. I hope you've made that church aware of what it's going to cost them to hire you."

Keene narrowed his eyes, wishing Brian were there so the man could see the dead seriousness on his face. "Don't worry about it. I've got that covered. They already know the amount, and they've agreed to pay it."

"Hey, you're smarter than I thought you were."

"But I also told them if the offerings they take every night don't measure up to the agreed-upon amount—"

"Not measure up? What about my—"

"Cool it, Brian. Let me finish. I told them they could go ahead and write out a check for the full amount and I would, in turn, make out a check to them for the difference and give it back to them, and they could consider it my gift to the church."

Brian laughed into the phone. "Wahoo! Good thinking, Keene. They get their little Easter pageant, I get my full commission, and you get a nice write-off! Good job, old buddy."

"Yeah, that should make everybody happy, and my tax man will love the idea."

"But what's with you, man? You don't go to church. I've heard you tell people you don't even believe in God. Why this sudden change and devotion to some church?"

Jane's adorable image immediately popped into Keene's mind. "You wouldn't believe it if I told you."

The next morning at exactly 8:45, the BMW moved into a parking space in the Randlewood Church parking lot.

❧

Jane was standing by the piano going over one of her solos when Keene entered the sanctuary. She stopped cold when she saw him, not yet feeling comfortable about singing in front of him. Not only that, her head was still spinning, almost as much as her heart, from the kisses in the parking lot the night before.

"Places, everyone." Ben tapped his pen against the microphone. "Let's get started." He turned to Keene, who was standing in the middle of the platform as if unsure where he should sit. "For now, why don't you have a seat there at the end of the fourth row, in the baritone section?"

Keene nodded and moved into the chair, shaking hands with those seated around him and giving them a friendly smile.

"Let's start on page thirty-nine," Ben told them, flipping the pages in his book. He motioned to Jane. "Your first solo is on the next page, Jane. Why don't you come on up to the microphone so you'll be ready?"

She cast a quick glance Keene's way as she moved into the aisle. Although she was still nervous about singing in front of him, her thoughts were on the kisses they'd shared, and her knees began to wobble. Finally, she moved into position, and the music started. She tried to concentrate, to become Mary as Ben had suggested, but with Keene so near she found it hard to do. *Lord, please settle my mind. I want to sing for You. Keep my mind focused on You alone, and may the words Keene hears as we sing* Down from the Cross *cause him to be aware of his sins and make him realize his need for You in his life.*

A calmness washed over her as she gazed at the words in the book in front of her, and suddenly she was Mary. The emotions Mary must have felt became her emotions. All thoughts of Keene disappeared, and the only face before her became the face of Jesus. When it came her time to sing, she opened her mouth and sang for her Lord.

>▲.

Keene stared at her, amazed at the quality of her lovely alto voice and the way in which she sang. Each note was crystal clear, her phrasing perfect. He listened carefully, knowing each word was coming from her heart. How many times had he tried to do the same thing? Sing an opera or a concert from the depths of his heart? And failed? Oh, perhaps the audience had not known it, but he had. It had been hard to muster up feelings for some of the roles he had sung. Meaningless stories and plots. Some of them silly and amazingly dull. Yet he had given them his all, but it had been with great effort. With Jane, there seemed to be no effort at all. Her singing came out that way because her emotions were sincere, pure, and he envied her. She was singing to God. The God she knew—and he didn't.

At noon, the entire group enjoyed the light lunch the women had provided, took a fifteen-minute break, and then went back to work. By four o'clock, they reached the place in the book that called for Keene's first solo.

"We'll skip this part until later," Ben said, motioning toward Keene.

Keene rose quickly. "I'm ready. There's no need to wait."

Ben motioned toward the microphone. "Great. Let's do it."

The pianist began, the choir did a short lead-in, and everyone waited breathlessly to hear the magnificent voice of Keene Moray.

six

Keene took a deep breath and, with a smile he couldn't contain, began to sing in a high-pitched, falsetto soprano voice.

Every choir member's eyes bugged out, and they stopped singing and stared at him. Even the pianist stopped playing. Other than Keene's ridiculously funny voice still singing, the sanctuary was engulfed in silence.

When it became apparent he could stand it no longer, he gave a booming laugh that echoed throughout the big room. "It's a joke, folks!" he said, a giant grin plastered across his face. "I wanted to break some of the tenseness I felt. Look"—he held out his arm and pinched it—"I'm human. Please don't treat me like some freak. I am one of you now. We're in this together."

Somewhere in the top row, someone began to applaud, and soon the entire choir broke out with laughter and applause.

"He's really funny!" Karen said to Jane. "You must have a blast working for him."

Jane gazed at Keene, her heart filled with admiration and pangs of love. "Yeah, a blast," she said, grinning, once again remembering how wonderful it felt to be held in his arms. "You can't imagine what a blast."

Ben gave the pianist her cue to start again, and this time the magnificent voice of Keene Moray sang the words with feeling and emotion. By the time he finished his part, tears flowed from the eyes of almost everyone in the choir loft, including Ben Kennard.

Karen dabbed at her eyes with her sleeve. "How can he sing

those words that way, with so much feeling—words right from the scripture—and not believe in God?"

"That's what I want to know." *Speak to his heart, God. As he memorizes each song, may his mind be filled with Your Word. I pray, through hearing and singing this music, Keene will turn to You. And, Lord Jesus, keep my witness pure. You know the temptations that face me every day I work with him. I—I love this man.*

"Got any plans for this evening?" Keene asked Jane as they walked to their cars. "I'd like to take you to dinner."

She couldn't help but smile. "I'd love to go to dinner with you—on one condition."

He tilted his head with a slight frown. "Oh, and what might that be?"

"That you'll go to church with me in the morning."

He tapped his finger on his lips thoughtfully. "I was planning to spend all day working on *Down from the Cross.*"

"We can go to the early service at 8:30."

He locked his arm in hers. "You drive a hard bargain."

She smiled up at him, trying desperately to keep from looking at his lips. "Take it or leave it."

He pulled her toward her car. "I'll take it. Wear something nice. I am taking you to Capriccio's on Pine Street. The food is exceptional, the service is unparalleled, and the atmosphere is very romantic. You will go crazy over their seafood. I'll pick you up at seven."

She gave him a coy smile. "Seven will be fine. That way you can get a good night's sleep and make it to the early service."

❧

Keene had not prepared himself for the lovely creature who greeted him at the door when he arrived at seven. Wearing a simple black sleeveless dress, a string of pearls about her slender neck, and a pair of high-heeled black strappy sandals that made her legs look fantastic, the woman standing before him, with her shoulder-length dark hair swept up into an elegant French roll, bore very little resemblance to the woman he'd left only a few hours ago. That woman had been wearing a ponytail, jeans, and a sweatshirt. This woman was a real knockout, and she smelled nice, too.

"I hope I look all right." She did a graceful pirouette.

Words failed him. He responded with a low, drawn-out whistle. "All right? You're gorgeous!"

"I–I could change. I have a blue suit—"

He latched on to her arm. "No! You're perfect the way you are. I just wish I'd brought a can of mace."

"Mace? Why would you need that?"

He tugged her close to him, wrapped his arm about her waist, and whispered in a low, husky voice, "To keep all the men at the restaurant away from you."

Her nervous laugh made him smile. Actually, just being with her made him smile. Until he came to Providence, he had smiled very little. Or at least honest smiles. He had put on more false, on-demand smiles than he cared to remember. It was part of his job. But an honest, all-out smile from his heart? There had not been many. Until Jane came into his life and into his heart.

When they arrived, the maître d' took them to their table, calling Keene by name. Jane, who said she rarely had seafood, asked Keene to order for her, then oohed and aahed over the lobster as she dipped each bite into the drawn butter. They laughed their way through a pleasant meal, and to Keene's mind the evening ended all too soon. As they walked through the dingy, dimly lit hall with its torn carpet and burned-out lightbulbs toward the apartment she shared with her ailing mother, Keene had a sudden urge to take her away from all of this. Show her the world he lived in. Give her the fine things of life she had apparently never had. But why? She deserved so much more, yet he could not remember a single time since he had met her that she complained about her living conditions. How different she was from the many other women he knew. Each day, his appreciation for Jane and her values increased, and he found her more alluring than ever.

"I will see you at church in the morning, won't I?" she asked him while they lingered in the hallway.

"You'll see me before that. I'll pick you up at eight. You surely don't expect me to attend my first church service by myself, do you?" He slipped his arm around her waist and hugged her to him as emotions he had never experienced before took hold of him.

She smiled up at him. "Then you'd better make that 7:30 if you want to go with me. I have to be there early. The choir always goes over its special a time or two before we go into the service."

He frowned. "I forgot about you singing in the choir. Does that mean I'll have to sit by myself?"

She looped her arms about his neck and gave him a light-hearted smile. "Just during the first part. After the offertory, we go sit with the congregation. I usually sit on the front pew. Since I sing in the choir, I'll have to stay until nearly noon. I'm sure you won't want to sit through all three services. I can catch a ride home with Karen."

"Front pew it is. I'll save you a seat." He gazed into her eyes, amazed at her simple beauty. There was no pretense in Jane's life. No facade. No cover-up. She was who she was, and he loved that about her. With Jane, he could relax—be himself. Be the real Keene Moray, not Keene Moray the performer, and it felt good.

"I—I guess we'd better call it a night. I'm sure Mom is waiting up for me. I'd like to introduce her to you, but she hasn't been feeling well lately. Maybe another time."

"I'm looking forward to. . ." He could no longer resist her cherry pink lips, and his mouth claimed hers in a sweet, gentle kiss. When she did not pull away, he allowed his kiss to deepen. The feelings that flooded over him were a total surprise. He had never felt quite like this before. These were not the kind of feelings the guys at the gym talked about when they discussed the women in their lives. These were weird and wonderful feelings. Feelings of love and passion and, yes, even protectiveness. He wanted to scoop her up in his arms and carry her off to some faraway island where she could be his alone, without the pressures of everyday life and the demands of the world. *What am I doing, holding her and kissing her like this?* He backed away slightly and tried to shake such foolish thoughts from his brain. Other than the job she performed each day for him and singing in the cantata, they had practically nothing in common. Not only that, but she was a devout Christian. Her whole life centered on God. He did not even believe in God!

"Keene, is something wrong?"

Her words brought him back to reality. "Wrong? No. I–I'd better be going." He pulled his arms from about her waist after planting a brotherly kiss on her forehead. "See you in the morning."

Looking confused and a little embarrassed, she unlocked the door and moved quickly into her apartment.

Keene watched the door close behind her, his mind in a muddle. Jane Delaney had really messed up his life.

All night he lay sleepless in his bed, staring at the ceiling. He promised himself there would be no more kissing. From now on, things were going to be strictly business between them. Well, not exactly business, but he could not, and would not, allow their relationship to go beyond friendly. For both their sakes. It was not fair to lead her into thinking there could be any future for them. Future for them? What a ludicrous idea. He was a well-known performer with a brilliant career. A star in the field of music. He had only begun to tap the possibilities that lay ahead of him. He did not need a wife, and certainly not children—not with his busy schedule and his lifestyle of travel and glamour.

Jane, on the other hand, seemed to have no further ambitions than to marry someday and have children. She had no interest in social status, beautiful clothing, fine homes, or the other things money could buy. Obviously, the biggest problem separating them was this crazy, all-consuming love and devotion she had toward the God he did not believe existed! Even if they were attracted to one another in a way neither of them would admit, how would they ever get around such an obstacle?

Very little was said between them on the way to church the next morning. Despite his original intention to stay and take her home, he let Jane insist on riding with Karen and left alone after the first service.

❧

With so much to learn in such a limited amount of time, Keene kept mostly to himself the next few weeks, closing up in his room all day, taking only minutes out for a quick bite of lunch at noon. Though they often laughed and joked with each other, Jane could feel the strain in their relationship. She loved this man, no doubt about it. "Why," she asked God every day, "would You bring Keene into my life? Didn't You know I'd fall in love with him?"

To glorify My name, child.

"How, Lord?"

Trust Me, Jane. Trust Me.

❧

Checking the calendar on her desk, Jane shook her head.

Only one week before the first public performance of *Down from the Cross*. So far, things were going quite well. Keene had his parts down pat, their first full dress rehearsal was scheduled for the next day, and every single ticket had been given out with hundreds of calls coming in from people who desperately wanted to attend but hadn't gotten their tickets earlier or who had just heard about it.

The church board was overjoyed with the response. Nearly every day since the word had gone out that Keene Moray would be performing the lead in *Down from the Cross*, there had been either an article in the newspapers or a blurb on TV or radio. Instead of having to call and ask for coverage, the reporters were calling them, clamoring for interviews and any interesting tidbits they were willing to give them. Every one of them expressed interest in doing a feature story about Keene.

She whirled her chair around at the sound of the office door opening.

"Jane, explain this to me."

She rose quickly.

He handed her his music book. "How could any man walk on water? I find it hard enough to believe that Jesus did, but it says here that Peter did, too."

She took the book from his hands, knowing full well the line to which he was referring. "Peter could only do it because Jesus told him to come to Him. When Peter took his eyes off Jesus, his faith wavered, and he began to sink."

Keene eyed her suspiciously, his brow creased. "You don't really believe all that, do you? Or that Jesus raised people from the dead?"

"Yes, Keene, I do believe it, and I believe all the other miracles we read about in God's Word."

"Then you're way more gullible than I am!" He shook his head while closing the book and stuffing it under one arm.

"It's not being gullible, Keene. I believe because I have faith that what God says is true."

He gave her a puzzled stare.

"God's Word says, 'Faith is the substance of things hoped for, the evidence of things not seen.' The entire eleventh chapter of Hebrews is filled with stories of faith."

"Taking things by faith seems kind of stupid. Like believing in fairy tales."

"Do you ever fly in a commercial airplane?"

"Of course. Who doesn't?"

"Do you personally meet the pilot before your plane takes off?"

"No."

"Do you ever board a plane without meeting the people who made that plane or those who serviced it at the airport?"

"You know I do."

"And you tell me you don't take things by faith?" A smile crossed her face as she gave his arm a playful pinch. "I rest my case, Mr. Moray."

He appeared thoughtful, his eyes locked with hers. "You really believe all this Bible stuff, don't you?"

She couldn't help but laugh. "Of course I believe it. I'm so *gullible* I even believe the part on the inside cover of my Bible where it says 'genuine leather'!"

He held the book out again. "How about the part where it says Jesus rose from the dead?"

Her expression sobered. "Yes, Keene, I do believe Jesus rose from the dead, and that He's sitting in heaven right now, at God the Father's right hand. And I also know He's preparing a place for me."

"A mansion? Like the words in one of the parts I sing describes?"

"Absolutely." *God, help Keene to continue to dwell on Your Word.*

"Remember that Bible you gave me? I've been reading it some. When I have a chance," he quickly inserted. "Some of it actually makes sense." He headed for the door but stopped and turned to her. "You know, it amazes me the way the people at your church work so hard. I mean, I have watched men building sets, some painting backgrounds. Women working tirelessly creating costumes. The choir members rehearsing hour after hour each week and never complaining. None of these people is being paid a penny, yet they work harder and with more dedication than any of the professionals I have worked with over the years. And to top it all off, they're nice! I like them."

The ringing of the doorbell brought a halt to their conversation. She rushed to answer it.

"Well, who are you?" the attractive woman dressed in a tight-fitting red suit asked, eyeing Jane from head to toe.

"I—I'm Mr. Moray's assistant."

Without being invited, the woman stepped into the living room and looked around. "Nice place, but certainly not as nice as his New York apartment, or the one he stays at when he's in London."

"May I tell him who is calling?" Jane asked, in awe of the woman's audacity, the way she waltzed in without even announcing who she was.

"Tell him his little Babs is here. Come to see him all the way from New York City," she drawled out in a Southern voice. Jane recognized both the name and the drawl instantly. Babs was one of the women who kept calling Keene.

He rushed into the room and took the woman by her hand. "Hey, Babs, what are you doing here? I wasn't expecting you."

Babs draped her arms about his neck and pressed her skinny frame against him. "I'm here to see you, sweetie. You haven't been returning my phone calls. I was afraid something had happened to you, so I just hopped on a plane and came here to see you."

Giving Jane a quick sideways glance, he grasped the woman's wrists and pulled her arms away from his neck. "You should have let me know you were coming. I don't have one free minute to spend with you. I'm. . .I'm in rehearsals."

Babs ran a manicured finger down his sleeve, lowering her lip in a pouting manner. "Babs needs to spend time with her Keene. She misses him."

Jane covered her grin with her hand. This woman was coming on so strong it was ridiculous. Surely, Keene could see through her. *Is this the kind of woman he is attracted to? Is this why our relationship has suddenly cooled off?* She swallowed the lump forming in her throat at the thought. *Relationship? What relationship? All there has ever been between Keene and me is a few kisses and an "I think I'm falling in love with you" comment during a weak moment, and even that I'm not sure I heard correctly. If there is any relationship between us, I'm afraid it's all one-sided.*

Babs, not to be discouraged, slid her arm into Keene's and pouted up at him again. "I'm hungry. Can't you take me to some nice place for lunch? You have to eat!"

He pulled free of her grasp and took a step away from her. "We're having lunch catered in. Pizza."

To Jane, the look on the woman's face was priceless. His answer seemed to take all the steam out of her unladylike advances.

"I'm sorry, Babs. I wish you'd called before coming to Providence." Keene sent another glance Jane's way, sucked in a deep breath, and let it out slowly, then focused his attention on Babs. "I hope you have shopping or other things to do while you're here, because I simply don't have a minute to spare for the next two weeks. My rehearsals are going to take all my time." He took hold of her arm and gently ushered her toward the door. "Please don't think I'm rude, but I must get back to work. Maybe we can get together next time I'm in New York."

Babs shot a glance over her shoulder and sent a frowning glare at Jane. "Does *she* have anything to do with your busyness?"

Opening the door for her, he gave Babs a stern frown. "I won't even dignify that question with an answer."

The woman huffed out the door without returning his good-bye, her stiletto heels clacking on the hallway's marble floor.

"I'm sorry you had to see that," Keene told Jane after he closed the door. "That woman has been driving me crazy for months. I have told her repeatedly to quit following me around! I had one arranged date with her when I was per-forming in London. That's it, but since then she has been calling constantly and turning up unexpectedly at almost all of my performances. She even turned up in Japan!"

"From the phone calls that come in every day, I'd say she's only one of your many admirers." Jane chuckled. "I hope they're not all like that."

He shrugged. "Sadly, most of them are. Spoiled little rich girls with time and money on their hands and overindulgent mommies and daddies to cater to their every whim. And to think I used to like that kind of woman."

With a grin, she tilted her head and raised a brow. "Used to?"

"Yeah, used to."

She wished she knew what that statement meant, but when he did not offer to elaborate, she decided to let it drop and get back to work.

☙

Keene stopped outside the closed office door on the way to his room, tempted to go inside and try to give Jane a better explanation about Babs's impromptu visit. But he decided against it and moved on down the hall. *What's with me?* he asked himself, settling down in a comfortable barrel-backed chair. *Not long ago, I considered Babs funny and charming, the life of the party. Now, with her pushy ways, she seems obnoxious. Her very presence repels me.*

He didn't have to ask himself that question a second time. He knew what was wrong with him. He was comparing all the women he had ever met with Jane, and all of them were coming up short. But why? What did Jane have going for her the others did not? Although he considered her beautiful, she was certainly no more attractive than most of the women who continually called him. Her wardrobe consisted of either jeans and a T-shirt or sweats. Those women were always beautifully coiffed and adorned in the latest Paris fashions. She mentioned she had taken a few college classes. Most of the others had graduated from prestigious women's colleges. If Jane outshone them, there was only one reason that made any sense. She was who she was, 24/7. No dishonesty. No put-on. No trying to impress people by pretending she was something she was not. Her life was pure, sweet, and innocent. And what made her this way? He hated to admit it, but her faith in God and her gentle ways were what made her beautiful.

⁂

The dress rehearsal went even better than Keene expected it would. Though he had not said anything to Jane or anyone else from the church, he had been quite concerned about working with a group of nonprofessionals. The idea of the cast showing up onstage wearing chenille bathrobes and Roman soldiers carrying cardboard swords covered with foil had terrified him. In some ways, he was putting his career on the line, particularly now that *Down from the Cross* was garnering so much media coverage and promised to get even more once the performances started. However, the costumes were nothing like he had expected. Whoever created them had done their research. Everything rang true to the times and the traditions, and anyone could tell by looking that no labor or expense had been spared. The costumes rivaled the most expensive, elaborately designed costumes in any of New York City's finest productions.

It was nearly five o'clock before Keene walked Jane to her car. "Long day, huh?"

She stretched her arms above her head and brought them down, letting her breath out slowly. "Um, yes, but a good one. I'm really excited about *Down from the Cross*. Not just because you are singing the part of Jesus, but also because I think the entire cantata has a wonderful message. It's my prayer that many in our audience will hear the plan of salvation through it and accept Christ as their Savior."

"You really do believe all of this, don't you?" The hurt look on her face told him his words had offended her.

"Keene," she began, her pale blue eyes filled with an unexpected intensity, "could you have been around me all these weeks and doubt my sincerity? You keep asking me that question. Yes, I do believe it. All of it! And I wish you did, too!"

He stepped in front of her and grabbed both her wrists. "Why does this always have to come back around to me? Has your God made you my keeper?"

Anger flared in her eyes, and she blinked away her tears. "Yes, I think He has! At least, He put us together so I could share my faith with you!"

His laugh came out haughtier than he intended, and he instantly wished he could take it back. "Next you'll be telling me God made me run that stoplight and ram my car into yours, breaking your leg!"

She lifted her face to his, glaring at him as she jerked her hands free. "He might have. He can do anything He wants!"

"You are incorrigible!"

"You're stubborn!"

"You're gullible!"

"You're blind!"

Nose to nose, Keene thought about the ridiculousness of their argument and how childishly they were both behaving, and he broke out in laughter.

Jane stared at him for a moment then joined in.

"We're quite a pair, aren't we?" he asked, still laughing as he whipped an arm about her waist and lifted her up in his arms, her feet dangling above the pavement.

She giggled and nodded her head. "I wonder if God is up there laughing at us."

He chuckled, too. "I don't know, but if He is, I hope He's watching!" With that, he set her down and planted a kiss on her lips. When she didn't protest, he gazed into her eyes then kissed her again as her arms willingly slipped around his neck.

When he finally released her and set her back down on the pavement, she gave him a long, hard stare he was not able to interpret. "Got any more names you want to call me?" he asked sheepishly.

"Yes, as a matter of fact, I do," she said, putting her fists on her hips. "Thoughtful. Talented. Handsome. Generous. A great kisser." A smile touched her lips. "Want me to go on?"

"No, it's my turn." He let loose a boisterous laugh and once again snatched her close to him. "You're beautiful. Kind. Caring. Smart. Funny. Terrific to be around." He suddenly turned serious. "And the best example of Christianity I've ever seen."

Jane reached up and cupped his cheek with her palm, smiling the sweetest smile he had ever seen on a woman's face, causing his heart to do funny things in his chest. "Keene, nothing you could have said would have pleased me more, except that you, too, want to accept God's plan of salvation for your very own. My prayer, since the day I met you, was that God would use me and my love for Him to reach you." She stroked his cheek with her fingertips. "God loves you, Keene, and so do I."

He stood mesmerized by her words while she climbed into her little car and drove away.

seven

Coral Mills, a longtime member of the church who was approaching her nineties, glanced at her watch. In only ten minutes, the first performance of her church's annual Easter pageant would begin. She reached across her daughter-in-law and took her son's hand. "I'm so glad you two could make it tonight."

Ralph Mills patted his mother's hand with a smile. "Me, too, Mom. I'm not that interested in the pageant, or whatever they call it, but I am really excited about hearing Keene Moray sing. Amy and I have been fans of his for a long time, but we've never heard him in person."

Amy's eyes widened as she peered around the crowded sanctuary. "I've heard the tickets have been gone for weeks. I'm sure glad you were able to get tickets for us, Mother Mills."

"So am I." Coral breathed up a prayer of thanks. *Lord, You know how long I have been praying for my son and his wife. They need You. Please, speak to their hearts through the music tonight. I so long to see them saved before I pass on. I'm trusting in You, God!*

Ralph glanced at the program in his hand then leaned across Amy. "Mom, I'd like to ask you a question. I don't claim to be a Christian, but I don't understand how come your church will allow a man to play the part of Jesus. Jesus was supposed to be perfect. How can you let a mortal man who is not perfect portray His part? Isn't that a bit sacrilegious?"

Coral smiled, glad he was considering such things. To her, it proved he was open. "Oh, son, the first year we decided to do an Easter pageant, there were all sorts of questions like this from our regular members. We didn't want to do anything that would bring reproach upon our Savior's name or the church's name, so we considered every conceivable complaint we might encounter and discussed it at great length. Your dear father served on the board at that time."

Ralph squeezed her frail hand. "I guess they must have decided it would be okay."

"Oh, yes. They decided it would be okay, but only after hours and hours of discussion and prayer. In the end, the board voted unanimously to go ahead with their plans. The church's sole purpose is to spread the gospel of Jesus Christ to all who would hear, to nurture and train Christians young and old, and to provide support and encouragement to one another. Our yearly pageants do that very thing. Thousands of people from our community attend these special events. Many of them have never even been in a church, except to attend weddings and funerals, and this is the only time they will sit and listen to God's Word. There is something about hearing it set to music and seeing it portrayed in costume with an appropriate setting that makes them see the reality of what actually happened two thousand years ago and how God's love and plan relate to them."

He gave her an adoring smile. "Thanks, Mom. I knew if anyone would know the answer, it would be you."

As the lights dimmed and the prelude began, the Mills family, together with twenty-five hundred others, settled back in their seats to enjoy *Down from the Cross*.

❧

Jane wanted to fade into the woodwork. She felt like this every time she sang before an audience. Ben Kennard always reminded his singers that being nervous before a performance helped them to sing even better. It meant they had to be dependent upon God to get them through it, rather than their own talents.

She had not seen Keene since two o'clock when he left his apartment, saying he had an appointment. Which seemed strange, since he had not written an appointment on his calendar. Well, no need to worry. If he hadn't made it to the church by now, Ben Kennard would be tearing his hair out.

She hurriedly took her place in the darkness onstage with the others, ready to sing *Down from the Cross* to their waiting audience. The orchestra finished the prelude and spotlights focused on a scene set high up in one corner where there appeared a group of Jewish leaders, donned in fine velvets and decorative hats, discussing what they were going to do about this man called Jesus who had caught the attention of the people.

When the upper lights dimmed, other spotlights flooded the stage, which was filled with people milling about the marketplace, shopping and visiting, with children running to and fro. Someone hollered, "Jesus is coming," and they all began cheering and waving palm branches high in the air. Jane, in her costume as one of them, waved her palm branch, too, straining for the first view of Keene as he entered, playing the part of Jesus. Though she'd been to all the dress rehearsals and sung *Down from the Cross* many times, she'd never experienced the sensations that overtook her when she and the others sang, "Hosanna, Hosanna, blessed be the Lord!"

He moved about the crowd in his long robe and sandals, smiling at people, lifting children and tousling their hair. The way he'd let his beard and his hair grow long over the past seven weeks, and the marvelous job the makeup people had done in bronzing his skin and applying touches of color around his eyes, had all changed Keene's appearance. In her eyes, he now looked more like the likeness she had envisioned of her Lord than like Keene. *Oh, Father,* she prayed, waving her palm branch with the others, *even though this man is not a Christian, use him to win souls. May everyone forget this is an earthly man and think about Christ.*

Though Keene never spoke a word in the first scene, he was a powerful presence onstage.

She hurried offstage with the others while the next scene shifted to the temple where people were exchanging their money. She watched from the wings while Jesus moved in quickly, asking them what they thought they were doing and reminding them they were making His Father's house into a den of thieves, ordering them to stop. When they did not, He overturned the moneychangers' tables. He did it with such passion, Jane found herself forgetting she had a costume change and had to hurry while the next scene, the one in which the Jewish leaders met with Judas to arrange Jesus' capture, played above the stage.

Moving onstage once more, she watched Jesus move about the happy crowd, smiling, healing the sick, making the lame to walk, the blind to see, casting out demons, even raising the dead to life again. It was clear Keene was no stranger to performing. His stage presence was flawless and every cue right on time.

By the time it came for Jane's first appearance as Mary, Jesus' mother, her heart was so full of God's love that she found herself eager to sing, with all the nervousness she'd expected gone. But as she stood on the stage waiting for her cue, Jesus entered, bleeding, battered, and beaten, limping and falling under the weight of the heavy cross He bore on His shoulder. The scene of her Lord suffering like that, the flesh on His back literally torn from His bones, was nearly too much to bear, and she found herself weeping, her chest heaving with each sob. When they led Jesus to the cross, Jane cried like she had never cried before, her heart breaking for the Savior who had bled and died for her. *Lord, I will never get through this without Your help!* But when she opened her mouth to sing, even though she could not stop crying, she felt God's presence, and she sang it to Him.

When she came to the last few lines of the song, Jane fell to her knees and, raising her face heavenward, sang, "How can this be happening? How can this be true? Can it be, dear Father God, that you are crying, too?"

Even though she had sung those words many times, they took on a whole new meaning. Through tears of sorrow, she fixed her gaze on the body of Jesus, sprawled out upon the cross while the soldiers began to hammer the nails into His hands and feet, one by one, the sound echoing across the great auditorium. Jane had to wonder how Keene felt, lying there with his hands and feet being anchored to the cross, the pounding of the hammer so close to his head.

When the soldiers finally finished their heinous deed, along with the other performers and the audience, she watched them raise the cross with its sign nailed above His head: *JESUS OF NAZARETH—KING OF THE JEWS.* There Jesus hung in agony and excruciating pain, stripped nearly naked, taking on the sins of the world. It touched her heart so deeply she had to close her eyes lest she faint.

Like a bolt of lightning, Keene's voice rang out, splitting the heavy silence. "Father, forgive them, for they know not what they do!"

Like the scriptures said, the soldiers began to mock Him and cast lots for what little clothing He had left. Jane moved instinctively toward the cross and fell at its foot, weeping as Mary would have wept, feeling many of the emotions Mary must have felt. The man singing the apostle John's part knelt beside her, wrapping an arm around her. Writhing in pain, Jesus lowered His head, His face nearly covered with blood from the crown of thorns pressed into His tender flesh, and asked him to take care of His mother.

"If Thou be the Christ, save Thyself and us!" one of the thieves hanging on the crosses on either side of Him called out sarcastically.

The other thief lifted his weary head and rebuked him, saying, "Dost thou not fear God? We receive the due reward of our deeds, but this man hath done nothing!" Then the man turned his face toward Jesus. "Lord, remember me when Thou comest into Thy kingdom."

With great effort and pain, Jesus turned to the second thief. "Today thou shalt be with Me in paradise."

Jane watched, and from her heart she whispered, "Oh, Keene, you are like the first thief, denying the existence and deity of God. Listen to what you are saying! Don't turn your back on Him, or like that thief you'll spend eternity in hell." But he was too far away to hear.

They moved through the other scenes, each one so special, so touching. When the last scene ended, showing Christ ascending into heaven, and the final song had been sung, Pastor Congdon moved to the center of the platform and extended an invitation to anyone who wanted to accept the risen Christ as their Savior. Hundreds of people moved into the aisles, crowding around the front, weeping and eager to commit their lives to God. Jane watched from the wings, breathing a prayer of thanks to her Savior for using this means to reach souls for Him and for letting her be a part of it.

❧

Coral Miller held her breath when, out of the corner of her eye, she caught sight of her son rising and extending his hand toward his wife, with tears rolling down his cheeks. Amy, too, was crying. But before the couple moved past her and headed for the altar of the huge sanctuary, Ralph bent and kissed

Coral's cheek, whispering how much he loved her and appreciated the prayers he knew she'd been praying for both him and Amy.

She watched her precious son slip an arm around his wife's waist and the two of them move forward to accept Christ as their Savior, her heart throbbing with grateful thanks to her Lord. For over forty years, she had begged God to bring her son into the fold, but he had never expressed the slightest interest in the things of God. Now, just months before her ninetieth birthday, God was answering her prayers.

Leaning back against the seat, Coral bowed her trembling head and folded her arthritic hands in prayer, tears running down her wrinkled cheeks. *Father God, You have blessed me more abundantly than I have had any right to ask. Thank You for letting me live long enough to see the deepest desire of my heart fulfilled—Ralph and Amy accepting You as their Savior. Lord, You can take me home anytime now. I'm ready to go.*

ða

Keene was waiting for Jane when she finally made her way to her car. She had stayed late to help counsel some of the young people who had come forward. She was surprised to find him there. The last time she saw him, he had been signing autographs for the many people who crowded around him after Pastor Congdon dismissed the audience.

"Well, we did it! Everything went off like clockwork. The members of Randlewood Church can be very proud of what they've done." He took her hand in his and gave it a squeeze. "You were wonderful as Mary. I knew you would be."

She sent him a shy smile. "Thank you." Though she was grateful for all the hours of practice he had put into *Down from the Cross*, she had to admit she was a bit turned off by his boastful tone. She had been so sure once Keene performed the part of Jesus, he would be so touched by the message he would fall to his knees and accept her Lord. But apparently it had not happened.

Patience, My child. Patience.

"You were amazing tonight, Keene. The audience thought so, too."

He gave her chin a playful jab. "I'm supposed to be amazing. I've had many years of practice, remember?"

"I mean. . .you sang with such meaning, I thought—"

"That I believed what I was singing?"

"Yes, I'd. . .I'd hoped so."

With a finger, he lifted her face up to his and gazed into her eyes. "Sorry, kiddo. I hate to disappoint you, but all I was doing was portraying a part and doing it the best I could. I still don't believe in God."

She blinked furiously, trying to hold back tears. "I'm still going to pray for you."

"By all means do, if it'll make you feel better, but don't count on any miracles." He grabbed her hand with a slight chuckle, linking his fingers with hers. "I'd invite you out for a cup of coffee, but I'll bet you're tired." He took her car key and opened her door. "Don't worry about coming in early tomorrow. I probably won't be in the office myself until about noon."

She nodded. "Thanks, but I'll be there long before that, and you're right. I am tired. I'll hold you to a rain check on that coffee."

"You've got it!"

❧

"Did you see your picture on the front page of this morning's newspaper?" Jane asked excitedly, waving the paper at him when he came into the office the next day. "And there's a wonderful article saying how you graciously stepped in when the lead singer was unable to perform due to his illness. They were quite complimentary about *Down from the Cross*, even mentioned how many people responded to the invitation to accept Christ."

He gave the paper a casual glance and began to shuffle through the mail. "That's nice. When you're finished reading it, put it in my publicity file."

"That's all you've got to say? That's nice?" She sent him a look of exasperation, upset that he had focused his attention on the mail and not on her words. "I was thrilled with the article."

He placed the mail back on the desk with a guilty grin. "I'm sorry, Jane. I have something else on my mind. I'm glad the writer of the article did a good job. What else did it have to say?"

She frowned. "What it failed to say could cause the church a real problem!"

"Oh? What's that?"

"They never mentioned that people needed to get a ticket to attend, and all of those free tickets have been given out! I talked with Pastor Congdon a few minutes ago, and although he wants a good turnout from the community, he is afraid many folks will come to the church expecting to get in, and there won't be any seats for them. We sure don't want to turn them away."

"He's right. It would be a shame for them to drive to the church only to find they have wasted their time. But I'm sure your pastor will figure out a way to handle things."

"I hope so. It also says you gave an amazing performance, and those lucky enough to be in the audience were given a real treat, as the Randlewood Community Church portrayed the true meaning of the Easter season."

Shivers assailed her when he sauntered close and circled her waist with his arm.

"It. . .it also talks about the beautiful costumes and sets and how they were all made by volunteers from the church who. . ."

She could feel his warm breath on her cheek. "Who spent many hours. . ."

She sucked in a gasp of air when his lips brushed her eyelid. "Who spent many hours working in. . ."

His lips trailed to her cheek, and she thought surely her heart would stop beating. "Working in the church annex. . ."

"Yes, go on, I'm listening," he whispered, lifting her hair and feathering the words against her ear.

"In. . .in the church annex, using their own tools and—"

He pulled her into his arms, and his mouth claimed hers, the newspaper falling to the floor. All her resolve to keep their relationship on a friendly basis dissolved into nothingness. She leaned into the strength of his arms, enjoying his kiss more than she knew she had a right to enjoy it. Enjoying Keene's kisses and letting her love for him escalate would only mean trouble and disappointment. She tried to back away, but he held her fast, his lips once again melding with hers.

"Don't pull away from me, Jane, please."

The phone rang once.

Twice.

A third time.

His arms wrapped around her even more tightly. "Let the machine get it." His voice was husky.

Placing her palms on his chest, with a prayer to God for strength to resist this man's charms, she pushed away and hurried to the phone, her hand going to her throbbing heart. "Ke—Keene Moray's office. This. . .this is Jane. How may—"

"Let me talk to Keene," a man's voice said, cutting into her salutation.

She covered the phone with her hand. "I think it's Brian."

Keene stared at the phone then took his time crossing the room to take it from her. "Hello."

By the time he finished his conversation with Brian, Jane had already started working at the computer, bringing his fan database up-to-date, and the spell that had come over them both had been broken. It was back to business as usual.

She finished her work and hurried home to fix supper for her mother and tend to her needs before heading back to the church for the second night's performance.

To her amazement, when she arrived at the church at six o'clock, she saw a number of panel trucks parked around the side door, with uniformed men scurrying in and out. The logo on their uniforms and the trucks said "Superior Audio and Video Services." What were they doing there? This close to performance time?

"Can you believe what's happening?" one of the wardrobe women asked while she sewed a new button on a costume. "They've actually installed huge television screens in the church gymnasium and the fellowship hall to take care of the overflow crowds. Last night alone, Pastor Congdon said they had to turn away over eight hundred people, and that did not count all those who called begging for tickets. Isn't God good?"

Jane nodded, trying to take it all in. "Yes, He is." She walked hurriedly up the steps to the gymnasium, meeting Pastor Congdon on his way down. "Oh, Jane. Glad you're here. Guess you've heard about the big screens they're setting up. After last night's performance and that wonderful article on the front page this morning, plus all the television and radio coverage we've gotten, the chairman of our board called an emergency meeting, and they voted to have the screens installed to take care of the overflow crowds we're expecting all week. Isn't that great? Just think of all the additional people who will see our cantata and be touched by the Lord."

She frowned. The magnitude of what was happening was overpowering. "But can we take care of all those people? Do we have enough counselors?"

"It won't be easy. My secretary has been on the phone all day, calling those who are qualified to be counselors and asking them to be here every night. Plus, don't forget we have a counselors' class going on right now, and although those people haven't received their certificates yet, they're trained and ready to go. That should give us at least another fifty. In addition, of course, there are the people like you, who sing in the choir, who are also qualified to lead them to the Lord. Beyond that, we will just have to leave it all in God's hands. Good thing we just added that new parking lot. We've even had to call on our college-age group to help the other guys direct traffic!" He headed on down the stairs after once again thanking her for bringing Keene to them and asking him to sing Jim's part. She leaned against the banister and stared off into space. *Lord, when You do something, You really do it in a big way!*

Even though they had expected it, people filled the sanctuary long before curtain time, with both the gym and the fellowship hall holding capacity crowds, some folks even sitting on the floor. Jane kept an eye out for Keene, but knowing he was probably in makeup, she went ahead and dressed in her costume. Though she had hoped to be over her jitters by now, she still found her hands shaking at the thought of singing before such tremendous crowds. But hadn't God come through for her the first night? Calming her and giving her courage? Of course He would do it again. After all, she was doing it for Him, and she knew He would never let her down.

Like she had done the night before, Jane stayed in the wings whenever she was not required onstage, watching and listening to each scene. The scene in which the religious leaders brought the harlot to Jesus especially touched her this night, when they asked Jesus what should be done with the woman who had been caught in sin. Those men were trying to trap

Jesus into answering and condemning Himself by His own words. He knelt and wrote in the imaginary sand, and Jane's heart stirred. When Jesus stood and took the harlot's hand, giving her a tender and loving smile, and said, "Neither do I condemn thee. Go and sin no more," Jane was not able to hold back her tears. How could Keene go through this scene and still ignore the truth of God's Word? *Don't you see, Keene? Don't you get it? God loves you and is willing to forgive you of your sins. Why, oh, why don't you let Him?*

Once again, when the pastor gave the invitation, the front of the sanctuary filled with those seeking forgiveness. With so many to counsel, Jane and most of the other members of the choir moved in to help. The leader assigned her to those in the church gymnasium. But when she passed through the lobby on her way up the stairs, she caught sight of Keene, surrounded by his many fans, smiling and signing autographs, and she felt such a burden for this man. *Why couldn't he have been one of those kneeling at the altar?*

She barely saw him Tuesday and Wednesday. With the studying and memorizing for *Down from the Cross* behind him now, he was spending most of his time closed up in his room, working on the new opera. Friday afternoon, he appeared in the office doorway saying he had an appointment and volunteering to drive her to the church that evening. She accepted, hoping to get another chance to talk to him about God's Word. If he didn't accept Christ soon, he would be on his way from Rhode Island, headed back to New York, and she would never have an opportunity to witness to him again.

On the way to the church, he chattered endlessly about the positive publicity the media had been giving their production and how many churches had been contacting his New York agent about him doing the same type of thing for them.

"I told my agent to let them know I don't plan to make a

habit of this sort of thing," he said with a chuckle, maneuvering the BMW into a parking stall. "This was a one-time deal, and I only did it because a friend asked me to."

"It must be very gratifying to know you're in such demand." Although her words were meant to be a compliment, with the inflection in her voice they did not come out that way.

He turned off the car and stared at her. "Was that a left-handed compliment?"

She forced a teasing smile. "I only meant. . .well. . .I have been answering your phone, you know. I am definitely aware of how many invitations you get. Brian keeps me well informed, too. He takes every opportunity to remind me you did this against his advice."

He chucked her under the chin. "Brian works for me, remember?"

She laughed with an exaggerated, "Touché! How well I remember."

Leaning closer, he asked, "Aren't you going to wish me luck with tonight's performance?"

"No."

He tilted his head quizzically. "You're not?"

"No, I don't believe in such a thing as luck. Good or bad. Nothing with God is happenstance."

"Oh? Knowing you, I should have realized that's what you'd say."

Again, Keene delivered a flawless performance. So did the choir and the soloists. Not that Jane wasn't still nervous. She was. But by now she knew her faith in God would see her through, and it did.

While standing onstage, watching Jesus serve the disciples at the Last Supper, Jane nearly lost her composure. The scene took on a reality she never expected. Knowing Judas was going to betray her Lord, she wanted to shout out to Him, to tell Him Judas had negotiated His life for a few coins, barely the price of a slave. But while Jesus sang to those assembled, declaring His love for them, she kept her silence. It was only a pageant. There was nothing she could do to change history, and even if she could, she would not want to. It was necessary for God to send His only Son to earth to die for the sins of man in order to redeem them. Judas, though he was a betrayer, was part of that plan.

Later, when Jesus led His disciples to the Garden of Gethsemane to pray and they all fell asleep, she wondered how those who were a part of that closely knit group, the ones who should have loved Him most, could have slept so easily knowing He would soon be taken from them.

She watched Judas betray Christ with a kiss, identifying Him as the one the soldiers were after, and the way Peter cut off one of the soldier's ears. She could not help it. She sobbed openly. How it must have grieved God to see His Son treated this way. Peter denied his Lord three times. How many times had Keene denied Him? Did Keene even care how many times he had denied God's call on his life? Did he not realize God had sent him to this very place, at this very time, that he might learn about Him and accept Him before it was everlastingly too late?

Clothed as Mary, Jane stood in the dressing room and lowered her head, once again praying for Keene's salvation.

In My own time, child. In My own time.

eight

Although Keene stayed in his room all morning and Jane had very little contact with him, she knew something was wrong. She sensed it. She could feel it in her bones.

A little before noon, when she asked him what he'd like for lunch and he told her, "Nothing," she knew she'd been right. An avid eater, Keene never missed lunch or any other meals. With two more performances to go, she knew he needed his nourishment.

"But I don't want any lunch," he told her in a firm tone when she knocked on his door for the third time. "I told you, I'm not hungry."

She turned the knob and pushed it open a bit, unsure how he would react to her invading his privacy. "Please, Keene, would you at least let me fix you a bowl of soup? I noticed you had a can of chicken noodle soup in the cabinet when I was looking for the cinnamon."

He yanked open the door and glared at her. "How many times do I have to tell you? I don't want anything to eat!"

"Okay, okay! I get the message!" She backed away, holding her palm up between them. "I'm just concerned about you, that's all. But if you want to get cranky about it, I'll get out of your hair." Lifting her chin in the air, she turned on her heel and strode off down the hall. "Just don't say I didn't offer!"

He followed her, catching up with her when she reached the office. "Look, I'm sorry! Give me a little slack, will you?"

She spun around, knowing she had fire in her eyes. Sometimes the man drove her crazy! "Give *you* a little slack?

How about you giving *me* a little slack? I only wanted to help you!"

He tried to place a hand on her shoulder, but she brushed it away.

"Okay!" He cupped his palm against his neck. "If you must know—I have a sore throat. I felt it coming on last night and gargled with some lemon juice before I went to bed, hoping it would be gone by this morning, but it wasn't. In fact, it's getting worse by the hour."

"A sore throat?" She frowned the way her mother used to do when Jane was ill. "You poor thing! What can I do to help? Did you call a doctor? Have you taken any antibiotics? What about throat lozenges?"

"I've tried all of those things already, and yes, I called my doctor. But my throat is tighter and sorer now than it was this morning when I got out of bed."

She began to wring her hands. "Oh, Keene, you should've told me instead of shutting me out."

"And have you worried about tonight's performance?"

She stepped up beside him and slipped her arms around his neck. "Of course I'm worried about tonight's performance, but it's you I'm worried about most of all. Do you think this may be from having to perform so many nights in succession?"

"I–I don't think so. My doctor—" He shrugged and paused midsentence. "Never mind."

Grabbing his hand, she tugged him toward the barrel-backed chair. "You sit right down here while I go fix you a lemon gargle. Fortunately, I bought some lemons at the store yesterday when you sent me to pick up some of those bagels you like so well."

"I know. I used one."

"I was planning on making a pitcher of fresh lemonade to

surprise you." She pointed her finger at him. "Stay. I'll be back in a minute."

When she returned, she had a cup of warmed lemon juice slightly diluted with water. She handed it to him. "Gargle."

Tilting his head with a grin, he said, "Yes, Mother."

She watched him take sip after sip of the lemon juice, gargling after each one. "Does it hurt very much?"

He nodded, wrinkling up his face after the last swallow.

Taking the empty cup from his hand, she leaned over him. "Let me look."

Turning away and rearing back from her advance, he frowned. "At my throat?"

She laughed. "Of course, at your throat! What did you think I meant? The empty cup?"

He covered his face with his hand, his embarrassment showing. "You really don't want to look at it, do you?"

"Of course I do. Now open your mouth and let me see."

Leaning his head back, he opened his mouth slightly.

"More."

He opened it a little wider.

"Keene! Open your mouth!"

She peered in when he finally obliged and screwed up her face. "It's really red! Are you sure this only started last night?"

"Okay, maybe two days ago."

"And you didn't say a word about it to anyone? Not even your doctor?"

"I kept thinking it would go away."

She leaned forward, hovering over him again. "I'm going to pray for you."

He bowed his head and shut one eye, peering at her with the other. "I suppose I have to close my eyes, don't I?"

"Yes, you do," she said, giggling. Then her tone turned serious. "Lord God, it's me—Jane—Your servant. I love You,

Father, and I come before You asking You to touch Keene's throat and make it well. There are two performances left. If he isn't able to sing, they'll have to be canceled, and the thousands of people who would have heard Your Word when *Down from the Cross* portrayed the last weeks of Jesus' life, His horrible death, and His resurrection will not hear it and acknowledge their need of You. I don't ask You so it will glorify our church, the choir, and all those who have worked so hard on the production, or for Keene. I ask it so Your name will be glorified. That through the words and the music many may come to know You. And if it be Your will, Lord, may Keene come to know You, too. He is such a fine man, and we praise You for sending him to us and for his willingness to step in and take Jim Carter's place. Touch him, God. Even now, heal His throat. Use the talents You have given him to magnify Yourself. I pray these things in Jesus' name, knowing You can answer prayer above and beyond what we ask or think. Amen."

❧

Keene listened to the prayers of the woman in front of him, her forehead resting against his, her words on his behalf touching his heart in a way he'd never known. *Can all this God stuff she keeps spouting at me be true? Is there really a God up in heaven with the power to heal His children if they ask Him to?*

No one had ever prayed for him like this before. Perhaps his mother had, but never in front of him. Never laid her hands on his shoulders and prayed so earnestly. And if he ever needed prayer for the healing of his throat, it was now. Now more than ever.

He opened his eyes when she said, "Amen," hoping she wouldn't see his tears. Rising slowly, he opened his arms wide, and she slipped into them, looping her arms about his waist and hugging him tight. "Thanks, Jane. I–I don't know if your prayers will help, but they sure can't hurt."

She raised misty eyes to his, and the concern he saw there melted his heart. "Oh, ye of little faith."

"I—I wish I had your faith."

She pressed herself against him, burying her head in his chest. "It's yours for the taking. All you have to do is believe."

"It. . .it can't be that simple," he murmured softly against her hair.

Again, she lifted misty eyes to his. "What's really keeping you from it, Keene? Pride?"

"Maybe. And I'm not even sure, if there is a God, that He'd want me."

"Wouldn't want you? Of course He wants you! He said, 'Whosoever will may come.' That is you, me, the guy down the street, the woman behind the counter at the grocery store, the greeter at Wal-Mart. Everyone. He isn't willing that any should perish but that all would come to Him." She reached up and cradled his cheek with her hand. "Be a man and face up to the fact that you're lost, and turn your life over to God. None of us knows what a day may bring. Tomorrow may be too late."

He folded her hand in his, bringing it to his lips and kissing her palm. "You really are concerned about me, aren't you?"

A tear rolled down her cheek as she gazed into his eyes. "Yes, Keene. I am truly concerned about you. You're. . .you're very important to me."

He stared into the pale blue depths of her eyes. He wanted so much to hold her and kiss her, but the reality of his sore throat hit him when he tried to swallow. The last thing he wanted to do was give his illness to her, so he held back. Looking at her longingly, he wished he could tell her how he really felt at that moment. But he couldn't. He knew, even if he told her that he loved her, she could not and would not accept that love. But he couldn't bring himself to lie to her either. To let her believe he accepted her God when he had not. From the beginning, he had been truthful with her. He could not start lying to her now. It would not be fair. "Keep praying for me, Jane. Who knows, someday I just might begin to believe in your God."

"I have to go now," she said, backing away and pulling free of his grasp. "The UPS man is coming to pick up some packages, and I don't have them ready." She motioned toward his bed. "Why don't you take a nap? It'll be good for your throat. I'll come back in an hour or so with another cup of lemon juice."

He gave her a shy grin. "You think your God needs the help of the lemon juice to heal me?"

She wagged a finger at him as she backed through the door. "He did make the lemons, you know!"

Keene watched her close the door then crawled into his bed and pulled the quilt up over him. His throat still hurt. He smiled, remembering her sweet prayer and the way she had knelt in front of him. Maybe this God thing would not be so bad after all.

At three, and again at four thirty, Jane brought warm lemon juice in to Keene, standing beside him until he had gargled with each drop. He almost hated to admit it, but his throat actually seemed a bit better.

She rapped on the door at five, saying she would see him at the church—if he felt like singing.

"I'll make it. I think the lemon juice is helping."

"The lemon juice or the prayer?"

From his place beneath the quilt, he snickered. "Both!"

At five thirty, he showered and dressed. Then he nibbled on the soft oatmeal bars and the fresh peach Jane had placed on a plate beside his bed after she reminded him he needed to get some food into his stomach.

By six-thirty, he was seated on a stool in front of a makeup mirror while Shirley Gordon, one of the beauticians who had volunteered her services each night, applied bronzer to his face.

"Shirley, you're a Christian, right?"

She stared at his image in the mirror and gave him a weird look. "Sure, why do you ask?"

"You do know I'm not, don't you? A Christian, that is?"

"Yeah, I heard that you told the folks in the choir you weren't." She went back to applying the bronzer.

"And you really believe Christ died for our sins?"

"Sure."

"So you admitted you were a sinner?"

She tilted his face toward her and appraised her work. "Had to. Everyone's a sinner."

He frowned. "What could you have done that was so bad?"

She screwed the lid on the makeup jar and stared at him. "Hey, it wasn't any one thing that I did that made me a sinner. It was everything I did that separated me from God. The biggest sin of all was rejecting Him. I can't believe I put off confessing my sins and accepting Christ as my personal Savior as long as I did." She picked up a pencil and began darkening his already dark brows. "Close your eyes."

"So you're telling me it made a real difference in your life?"

"Difference? I cannot tell you what a difference. Not that everything has been rosy since then. It hasn't. We live in a mixed-up world with all sorts of temptations. Accepting Christ does not make you perfect. Far from it. But it does make you a sinner saved by grace."

He swiveled his chair toward her and grabbed her wrist. "Then why, Shirley? Why would anyone want to be a Christian?"

She paused thoughtfully, the pencil still in her hand. "Do you remember when you were a little boy and fell down and skinned your knee? Who did you run to?"

"My mother, of course."

"How about when you needed something?"

He thought about it before answering. "My mother."

"Who did you run to for comfort when the kids teased you or you felt bad?"

"My mom."

"And what did she do?"

He gave her a scowl. "She comforted me, of course, and told me everything was going to be okay."

Shirley leaned over him and dabbed her finger at his brow, removing a smudge. "Those are just a few of the things God does for us. He is always there waiting to kiss our boo-boos, supply our needs, and comfort us when we need comforting. My dad died when I was fifteen, and you know what? God promised to be a Father to the fatherless, and He was. Whenever I needed my dad's advice, I would go to my heavenly Father in prayer, and He always came through for me. My mom, bless her heart, missed him, too. God also promised to be a husband to the widows. I'm not sure she would have made it without my dad if God hadn't been there for her."

She pulled a tissue from the box on the counter and dabbed at her nose. "I'm a single mom, Keene, and I've had some rough times, believe me. There were many days when I was attending cosmetology school that I did not have the money for next month's rent. But I turned to God and laid my needs at His feet, and somehow the money always came in just in time. He supplied my every need and still does. He tells us to cast all our cares on Him, and do I ever!"

Keene gave her a warm smile, appreciative of her willingness to open up her heart to him. "I guess you'd highly recommend Him, right?"

Her thumbs-up appeared in the mirror. "Oh, yes, I highly recommend Him." With a wink, she pulled the plastic covering from his shoulders. "And if you're as smart as I think you are, you'll accept Him, too."

He rose and leaned toward the mirror, turning his face first one way and then the other. "You do a good job."

"Thanks. Oh, by the way, someone told me some big wheel is in the audience tonight, all the way from New York City."

"Big wheel?"

"Yeah. I think he said he was an editor from the *New York Times*. Probably came all this way to hear you."

Trying to appear nonchalant, Keene shrugged. "Could be."

&

Jane elbowed her way through the many people backstage and headed for Keene's dressing room, a classroom that had been assigned to him, anxious to check on his throat.

"Jane!" The voice came from somewhere in the throng of people near the wardrobe racks.

"Oh, hi, Pastor," she said, turning with a smile. "Can you believe the crowds that've been coming every night?"

"Amazing, isn't it? Sure glad the board voted to add those big screens. We never would never have made it without them, and the free-will offerings every night have been amazing. Even with the additional expense we've acquired, we'll more than adequately meet our budget, even after we pay Mr. Moray the full amount."

"Have you seen Keene?" she asked, scanning the wardrobe racks.

"No, but have you heard the managing editor of the *New York Times* is in the audience tonight? He called me when he arrived in town, asking for a ticket."

"No, I hadn't heard. I wonder if Keene knows he's here." She moved on past him, motioning in the direction of the classroom where she hoped to find her boss. "I'll be sure and tell him."

"There you are!"

Jane smiled warmly when Keene approached her. "How's the sore throat?"

He tugged her away from the hubbub of the busy wardrobe area toward the hall. "Better! Not gone. But better. I think the lemon juice gargle did it."

She lifted a questioning brow, a smile playing at her lips.

"Maybe the prayer," he conceded. "Guess we'll never know which."

"You'd better make sure to use that lemon juice gargle again tonight before you go to bed, and it wouldn't hurt to use it several times tomorrow. Maybe you had better hold your singing back a bit tonight. We don't want you to strain your voice and not be able to sing for tomorrow night's final performance." She snapped her fingers. "Oh, that reminds me. Did you know some editor—"

"Is going to be in the audience tonight? Yes, I heard about it when I was in makeup. If it's the guy I think it is, he's a pretty tough critic. I had better pull out all the stops tonight. I sure want a good review."

"But your throat!"

"I'll be careful, Mommy. I promise."

"I'll be praying for you," she hollered after him, watching him disappear into the crowd. She glanced at her watch then checked her makeup and garment in the full-length mirror mounted on the wall near one of the long wardrobe racks. *It's time to get onstage. The performance will begin in five minutes.*

Jane took her place after breathing a quick prayer for Keene, asking God to continue to place His healing hand on Keene's throat. She also prayed for the audience members, that God would open their hearts and minds while they listened to the gospel set to music.

Later in the performance, when it came time for the ascension scene, Jane hurriedly found a place in the wings where she had a full view of the stage. On each of the other six nights, she had been so busy helping everyone remove their costumes and hang them on hangers after her last time onstage, she'd missed it. The big platform was still clothed in darkness.

Suddenly a blinding light flashed, and in the center of the stage, Jesus appeared on a mountaintop, adorned in a pristine white robe, His arms stretched out wide, His countenance radiant. As He stood there, His face lifted toward heaven, the narrator's voice recited John 5:24. "Verily, verily, I say unto you, He that heareth my Word, and believeth on Him that sent me, hath everlasting life, and shall not come into judgment; but is passed from death unto life." When he finished, Christ ascended up into heaven.

On a small platform suspended up near the high ceiling, a spotlight trained on three trumpeters who heralded Jesus' entrance into heaven. Then a deep male voice boomed out dramatically over the speakers, "This. . .is my beloved Son, in whom I am well pleased."

On each of the previous six nights, she had thought Keene's performance could not have been improved. But tonight, even with his sore throat, he had outdone himself. Surely, it was because God, the Great Physician, had answered prayer and touched him. Then she remembered the New York editor. Could Keene have done his best for that man? And not for God?

She changed out of her costume and hurried to the gymnasium to help the other counselors, trying to put her crazy suspicions out of her mind. But when she pushed her way through the huge foyer, there was Keene, all smiles, standing with the man in avid conversation, nearly ignoring the many thronged around him seeking his autograph. She wanted to run off to some private place and cry. One more night. Just one more night. *God! Please!*

By the time the last person had left the gymnasium and Jane and some of the other women had helped the men straighten the chairs for the Sunday evening performance, the sanctuary was deserted. She cut through the semidarkened auditorium on her way toward the side door, but when she passed by the altar, she felt led to fall to her knees and pray for Keene.

Assuming she was alone, she folded her hands and lifted her eyes to the beautiful stained-glass window that graced the front of the church. She stared at the image of Christ knocking at the door, her heart clenching within her, and she began to pray aloud. She thanked God for bringing them through the past seven performances, for all those who had come forward to accept Him, and for touching Keene's throat. She thanked Him that her mother had felt well enough to stay alone in the apartment each evening. She praised Him for the way He led the church board into asking Keene to sing in Jim's place.

"Keene." Just saying his name sent a tingling flood of emotions wafting through her. "Lord, I'm so in love with this man it hurts, and I'm confused," she added. "At first, I thought I was in awe of him and his beautiful voice, but now I know that's not the reason. While I love his voice, it's not what drew me to him. It's the man, Father. Keene himself. Why did You let him come into my life? Didn't You know I'd fall in love with him?"

She pulled a tissue from her purse and blotted her eyes. "I don't care that he's famous. I don't care that he has fashionable apartments in both New York and London or a fancy car. I—I just wish he could love me the way I love him. But,

Father, the thing I long for most is that he would yield himself to You. God, I only want what's best for Keene."

⁂

Hearing a voice, Keene held his breath when he returned to the church to retrieve the briefcase he had forgotten. Someone was kneeling at the altar! He pressed himself into the shadows of the dimly lit sanctuary, remaining motionless, not wanting to interrupt. Not even intending to listen until he heard his name mentioned by the person who was kneeling in prayer just yards from where he stood. It was Jane!

What? What did she say? She loves me? He took a cautious step forward, cradling his hand to his ear. *And she wants only the best for me?*

He continued to listen, barely moving a muscle, until she finally rose and moved slowly across the floor's carpeted surface toward the side door, dabbing a tissue at her eyes. Thankfully, she hadn't seen him. He lingered a few more minutes, his gaze locking on the stained-glass window of Christ standing at the door knocking. She had explained its meaning to him that first Sunday he attended the morning service and how it symbolized Christ standing at the door of our hearts. She told him how we have to open that door ourselves, from the inside, since there is no handle or knob on the outside. Sometimes, since he had been singing the part of Jesus, he had even felt that knock on his heart's door. But how? How could that be? He didn't believe in Jesus!

Sleep eluded him that night, no matter how many sheep he counted. The words of *Down from the Cross* filtered through his mind, mingled with the conversation he'd had with the New York editor, Jane's lovely face, and the scripture verses he'd read in the Bible she placed on his nightstand the first week she came to work for him. Before he came to Providence, he'd never thought of himself as a sinner, much less felt the need to confess those sins to God. A God he did not believe in. But being around Jane and the people of Randlewood Community Church made him wonder. *What if they are right? What if there really is a God, and I am turning my back on Him? Maybe I should consider this confession thing. I might even talk to Pastor Congdon about it sometime.*

But why? His time in Providence was about to come to an end. In a few weeks, he would be going back to New York City. Back to his old life of exciting performances, extravagant parties, lavish social events, and. . .and. . .boredom. If he were honest with himself, he would have to admit he'd had more fun working with Jane, listening to her tinkling laughter and sharing deli sandwiches and pizza for lunch, than he ever had at one of those stuffy parties. It did not make sense! Jane had so little to offer compared to the wealthy, high-society women who frequented those parties. Why, when he was with her, did he feel like a teenager on his first date?

Maybe once this pageant is over, Jane and I can get better acquainted. So far, we have been on her turf. Maybe that is the reason I find her so alluring. Flipping onto his side, he pulled the covers about his neck with a smile of satisfaction. *If she were on my turf, perhaps I would not find her quite so attractive.*

Then he remembered something Jane had said. "I could never have a permanent relationship with a man who doesn't share my faith."

nine

At seven the next morning, Jane phoned Keene's apartment to check on his throat. When he answered on the fourth ring with a sleepy "Hello," she thought about hanging up.

"I'm concerned about you. How's the throat?" She could almost see him running his fingers through his hair, squinting at the clock to check the time.

"Still sore, but improved slightly."

"I. . .I take it you're not going to church this morning?"

A big yawn sounded on the other end of the line. "Naw, I thought I'd sleep in. It's been a pretty grueling week, and I had a hard time getting to sleep last night."

"I'll see you tonight then."

Another exaggerated yawn. "Why don't I pick you up? It's right on my way."

"I hate to impose."

"No imposition. You know better than that. I'll pick you up at six. Okay?"

"Sure. I'll see you at six. And, Keene. . ."

"Yeah?"

"Nothing."

She was already waiting by the curb when he arrived a few minutes before six. He gave her a pleasant smile as he leaned across the seat and pushed her door open. "Hey, you're looking nice tonight."

"Thanks." She glanced down at her new jacket. She rarely wore anything this flamboyant, but she liked it and hoped he would, too.

"Looks good on you."

She felt herself blushing.

On the way to the church, they talked about everything but what was uppermost on her mind.

By the time they reached the church parking lot, it was already full, and Keene had to park on the street. "Looks like we're going to have another capacity crowd tonight." He took her hand as they walked toward the church. "I've got to get into makeup. Shirley is expecting me."

"Yeah, I'd better hurry, too. I promised the wardrobe lady I'd help her again tonight. Maybe I'll stop by your dressing room after I change into my costume."

She watched him as they entered the doors, and he moved on down the hallway, whistling some unfamiliar tune while he walked.

Jane helped the busy woman by checking over the costumes and making sure they were in the proper order on the racks then changed into her own costume and waited her turn at the women's makeup table. After she finished there, she headed for Keene's dressing room. She had to talk to him. By the time she entered, he was in full makeup and wearing the soft beige robe and pair of sandals for his first scene, Jesus' triumphal entry.

He slipped his arm about her waist. "I'm about ready to begin my warm-up. Are you here to check on my throat or to wish me good luck?"

With a heavy heart and a sigh, she forced a smile. "Actually, neither. I figured if your throat was still bothering you, you would have said something about it by now. And remember? I don't believe in luck, good or bad."

"Oh, yes, I forgot about that." He gave her a grin and wiggled his brows. "So that means you came to hear me warm up?"

"I love hearing you warm up, but I had another purpose in

coming, Keene." Her heart pounding furiously, she gazed up into his eyes, hoping he would see her love for him and not be offended by what she was about to say.

"What is it, Jane? You're trembling." His voice was kind and filled with concern.

"I—I hardly know where to begin."

With his free hand, he brushed a stray lock of hair from her forehead. "Just say it. You know you can tell me anything."

She gazed into the depths of his dark brown eyes, promising herself she would not get emotional on him. "First, I have to tell you how wonderful it's been working for you these past few months. You've treated me with a kindness and gentleness I never expected."

"You've been a terrific employee. No one could've done a better job or been more dedicated than you."

"Then you stepped in, at great personal sacrifice, to sing Jim's part when your life was already full, learning and preparing for a new opera."

He bent and gently kissed her forehead. "No one twisted my arm. I did it willingly. For you."

"And you'll never know how much I appreciate it."

"But that's not what you want to talk about, right?"

"No, not exactly, but I'm leading up to it." She ducked her head shyly. "Since the day I started working in your office and you told me you didn't believe in God's existence, I've been praying for you." She lifted her gaze to his once again, feeling the need to look him directly in the eye when she bared her heart. "You are a fine man, Keene. Honorable. Respectable. And certainly talented. We have all been in awe of your breathtaking performances. Because of you and the way you have sung the part of Jesus the past seven nights, all of us have been drawn closer to our Lord. You've made us see how He suffered and bled and died for us."

He planted a soft kiss on her cheek. "I've done my best. I've given it my all, Jane."

"I–I know you have, but. . ."

"But what?"

"But if you don't believe in God, that also means you don't believe in Jesus. And if you don't believe in Jesus, then you must not believe in Easter." When he did not respond, she twined her hand in his, glad he had not seen fit to argue the point with her.

"The message of Easter isn't simply a story filled with symbolism and interesting thoughts. Everything portrayed in our Easter presentation actually happened to real people. God *did* send His only Son to earth. Christ *did* die a cruel death on the cross, taking our sins upon Himself. He *did* rise again and ascend into heaven to take His rightful place at His Father's right hand, and right now He's preparing a place for His children as He said He would."

"I never—"

"Let me finish, please. There's so little time left, and I have to say these things to you."

Giving her a weak smile, he remained silent.

"Each night, hundreds of people go to the front of the auditorium, Keene, to repent of their sins and accept Christ as their Savior because of seeing their need of God in their lives through your performance. I–I can't understand how you can sing the words and portray the part of my Savior like you do without it affecting you." She paused and caressed his cheek with her hand. "Is your heart so jaded and hardened by the world you can't feel the emotions your singing evokes in others?"

"Is that what you think? That I'm jaded?"

"I honestly don't know, but I'm so concerned about your soul. Promise me, tonight, as you sing each note, you will listen to the words with your heart. God loves you, Keene. I love you. Our pastor and choir director love you. The members of this church have learned to love you, and we've all been praying for you. Not for Keene Moray, the famous man who graciously bailed us out when our soloist became ill, but for Keene Moray, the caring man who has become our friend."

"But you—"

"Shh." She put a finger to his lips. "When you're up there hanging on the cross tonight, I'll be kneeling at your feet portraying the mother of Jesus, and I'll be praying for you, Keene, as I've never prayed before. Begging God to make you come to the realization that you are a sinner and to melt your hardened heart. He wants you for His own. Remember the stained-glass window in the sanctuary? And how, though Jesus is knocking, He is unable to open the door because it has to be opened from the inside?"

He nodded. "I remember."

"Only you can open that door, Keene. That decision is up to you alone. No one else can open it for you. Think hard before ignoring His knock." After standing on tiptoe and kissing his cheek, she withdrew her hand and backed away slowly, her eyes still fixed on his handsome face, now bronzed with makeup. "The Easter story isn't just a pretty story filled with symbolism, lovely white Easter lilies, and beautiful music. It goes much deeper than that. It is the truest love story of all time. God loves you, Keene. I love you, too, and I want the very best for you. That best is Christ."

Jane turned and moved out the door of his dressing room, knowing she had done all she could and God was the God of miracles. Surely, it would take a miracle to make Keene swallow his pride and admit he was a sinner.

Pastor Congdon caught hold of Jane's arm as she moved into the wide hallway. "Is Keene still in his dressing room?"

"Yes, he is." Blinking hard, she turned her head away and scurried on down the hall.

ﮐ

Keene stood staring at the open door. He had never seen Jane this emotional.

"Keene. I'm glad you're still here." Pastor Congdon hurried into the little room. "I'd like to pray for you before tonight's performance."

"Ah. . .sure. That'd be fine." *What is this? Stack it on Keene night? First Jane. Now Pastor Congdon?*

"Good. Would you kneel, please?"

Without replying, Keene lowered himself to one knee and bowed his head, feeling like a marauder in front of this godly man, Jane's accusing words fresh in his mind.

"Lord," Pastor Congdon began, placing his hands on Keene's shoulders. "I come to You tonight asking that, through this man who is so willingly giving of his time and talents, You will perform a great and mighty work. Use his voice as an instrument to speak to hearts, make Yourself real to those in our audience who have never accepted You as their Lord and Savior, and bring them to Yourself. Bless Keene, I pray, and may he feel the power of the prayer that has gone up for him. And most of all, may He feel Your touch upon his own life. Amen."

His hand still on Keene's shoulders, Pastor Congdon said with great sincerity, "You're a fine man, Keene. I am sure God has a special plan just for you. Thank you for everything you've done for us."

Keene rose slowly, his eyes fixed on the man's hand as it was extended toward him with a smile. "Thanks, Pastor Congdon," he muttered nervously, the prayer nearly overwhelming him. These people really cared about him. He reached out and shook the pastor's hand. "Being here, working with you and the fine people of this church, has been a wonderful experience I won't soon forget."

Suddenly the overture sounded. Glancing at his watch, Pastor Congdon headed for the door. "Guess you'd better get onstage. Remember, I'll be praying for you!"

"I will, and thanks." *It seems everyone is praying for me.*

ꝭ

Putting on her Mary costume for the final time, Jane couldn't believe how quickly the week of performances had passed. Soon this year's Easter presentation would be over, Keene would be going back to New York, and she would be looking for a job.

But in some ways things had been different tonight. In each scene in which Keene had appeared, she noticed a difference in him. He had seemed more intense, more involved than she remembered him being the past seven nights. Was this the way it always was for him on the closing night of a performance? Knowing it would be the last time he would sing the part, did he put more of himself into it than on the other nights?

She moved into an area at the edge of the set, waiting for her turn to enter. Suddenly, just a few feet from where she stood, Keene appeared as Jesus, His body bowed beneath the weight of the cross. She listened to the words of the narrator reading passages from Isaiah as Jesus moved onstage. "He is despised and rejected of men; a man of sorrows and acquainted with grief. Surely He bears our sorrows, and with His stripes we are healed."

Jesus stumbled and fell, and it was as if a dagger were plunged into her heart. How could her Lord have been treated this way? When He had done nothing but come to save people from their sins?

Stepping forward, she followed Him up the hill to Calvary,

aching for the deep wounds His body bore from the many beatings He had suffered, the thorn of crowns piercing His brow, the blood running down His forehead and into His eyes, watching while the soldiers spat upon Him and jeered Him, shoving Him and making a mockery of Him. The script called for her to pretend she was upset and crying, but there was no pretense in the emotions racking her when she beheld her Lord suffering so. She could not hold back the flood of tears that overcame her. As Mary, she screamed out for them to stop!

But. . .they didn't stop.

Someone, a man from the throng that had assembled, took the cross upon his own shoulders when Jesus fell and carried it for Him, placing it where the soldiers directed.

Then, shoving Jesus down, showing Him no mercy, they placed Him on the cross, pulling his arms open wide while they held him there.

As it neared time for Jane to sing, she felt sure she would not be able to utter a word. She watched, feeling pain for her Lord, her breath coming in short, quick gasps and her chest heaving with each sob. But knowing she must do it for God, she pled with Him for the strength and the voice to go on. Moving closer to Jesus and lifting her face heavenward, she began to sing. With tears flowing down her face, she raised her voice to God. By the time she reached the final lines, she was weeping so hard she could barely get the words out, and she had to pause to catch her breath. *Sing it as Mary would sing it, Jane.* Ben's words, the words he'd said to her that first night they'd practiced her solo, came back to her. *For these few minutes, you are Mary, the mother of Jesus. Be her. Respond the way she would respond. Weep as she would weep. Cry out the way she cried out. Forget about the audience. Do this for Him, Jane. Your Lord. Your God. The One who took your sins upon Himself and died on the cross for you. Think of His pain, His agony as He hung there on the cross as Mary would have thought of it. Take on her personality. Her demeanor. And yes—her burden. If you cry— so be it! If you have to stop and compose yourself before you can go on—so be it! Become Mary, Jane! Forget who you are, and be who God wants you to be at that moment. Mary, the mother of Jesus, and sing it from the depths of your heart.*

Without orchestral accompaniment and holding her hands up to God, she sang the final two lines with all the emotion she had tried so hard to keep tucked inside.

"How. . .can this be happening?

"How. . .can this be true?

"Can it be, dear Father God"—Help me, Lord!

"That You are crying, too?"

The sound of the first nail being driven through Jesus' hand echoed throughout the sanctuary, the entire room falling into a riveting silence. Jane cringed at the sound.

Then the second nail was driven into His other hand, and it was as if she herself could feel the pain.

The soldier with the hammer stepped over Christ's limp and bleeding body and moved to His feet, securing one foot to the upright beam with a third nail. An audible gasp swept over the audience, many people turning their heads away.

The hideous sight made Jane sick to her stomach as the fourth nail pierced His other foot, anchoring it, too, to the beam. The sound penetrated her very bones. She would never forget it.

She leaned forward on a trembling hand, trying to get a look at Jesus' face as the soldiers moved in and lifted the cross into an upright position with Jesus hanging there. The sight was nearly too much to bear, and she wanted to turn her head away, but instead she kept her eyes fastened on Jesus' face, the reality of what He had done for her overpowering. Were those actual tears trailing down his cheeks? There was something in the expression on Keene's face. Something she had never seen before. A tenderness. A longing she had never witnessed, and her heart nearly burst with both love and pity for this man. He had so much and yet so little. *Speak to him, Lord!* her heart cried out.

"All we like sheep have gone astray," the narrator's words came slowly over the microphone. "We have turned, every one, to his own way, and the Lord has laid on Him the iniquity of us all."

Just as he had done every other night, Jesus lowered His head and tenderly asked the apostle John to take care of His mother.

Then one of the thieves hanging on a cross beside Him called out sarcastically, "If Thou be the Christ, save Thyself and us!"

Like they had rehearsed it, the thief on the other cross lifted his weary head and rebuked him. "Dost thou not fear God? We receive the due reward of our deeds, but this man hath done nothing!" Then, with great effort, he lifted his face toward Jesus. "Lord, remember me when Thou comest into Thy kingdom."

Gasping for air and in terrible pain, Jesus turned to the second thief, His mournful gaze fixed on the man.

Jane stared at Keene, waiting for his response, but he simply continued to look intently at the man, his chest heaving up and down as if he could not catch his breath.

The soldiers looked at one another, their faces filled with question.

One of the soldiers whispered, "Today thou shalt be with Me in paradise." But the man's helpful cue was ignored as Keene continued to stare at the thief, his eyes almost glassy.

From offstage, the stage manager called out in a low voice,

"Today thou shalt be with Me in paradise."

But he, too, was ignored.

A buzz circulated through the audience. Something was wrong!

What was happening?

Why wasn't Keene saying his line? Surely, Keene Moray, the man who had sung many difficult parts to thousands of people all over the world, had not forgotten his lines. And if he had, why wasn't he taking his cues when they were repeated for him?

"Keene," Jane called out to him in a guarded voice. "Say your line!"

But he continued to hang there, his deep guttural breaths the only sounds coming from him and echoing out over the sanctuary's powerful speakers.

ten

It was all Jane could do to keep from shouting out the line to him. Off to one side, she noticed Ben slip onto the stage, an old robe from the wardrobe rack slung over his back to cover his street clothes. Cupping his mouth with his hands, he said in a lowered voice, "Keene! 'Today thou shalt be with Me in paradise.' Say it!"

Still no response.

The orchestra stopped playing, and all eyes fixed on Keene, battered and bleeding, his arms sagging with his body weight as he hung on the cross.

Once again, Ben called out. But still Keene did nothing but stare blankly at the thief hanging beside him, his chest rising and lowering as he sucked in deep breaths of air.

For the first time, Jane realized his tears were not only real, but he was sobbing from the depths of his being. Staying low, she crawled to the foot of the cross and, looking up at him, said in a pleading voice, "Keene! Say your line, please; everyone is waiting!"

As if he had suddenly come back to reality, he turned his head slowly and gazed down at her.

"Please, Keene," she implored softly, brushing away the tears from her cheeks. "Please."

Next he turned his head from one side to the other, taking in each face on the stage. Then his attention went to the soldiers who were standing at his feet, looking up at him with widened eyes, their faces filled with confusion.

"Get me down," he said in a whisper.

The soldiers looked to one another with bewilderment.

"Get me down."

The lead soldier looked toward Ben for direction.

With a frown, Ben shook his head. "Don't listen to him."

"I said, get me down," Keene said a third time, tugging on the fetters that held his arms.

"I think we should take him down," one of the taller soldiers told the others. "Maybe he's having a heart attack."

"No, don't!" another said. "Not without Ben saying it's okay."

With beads of sweat now covering his tired face and his body perspiring visibly, Keene took several more deep breaths. "Take me down from this cross."

Ben hunched over and moved to the foot of the cross. "We can't, Keene. It will ruin the cantata. Say your line."

Keene lifted his eyes heavenward, and on his face was a look of sheer torment.

Apparently forgetting his plaid shirt and khakis, the stage manager hurried to stand beside Ben. "Keene, are you okay? Do you need a doctor?"

A murmur went through the audience. Some began to stand, their curiosity getting the better of them. Others fell on their knees by their chairs, praying, while others simply sat staring.

"Get—me—down—from—this—cross—now," Keene said in a firm voice, again struggling against the cords binding his wrists and feet. "I have to get down from this cross! Now!"

Ben and the stage manager looked at each other then motioned for the soldiers to take him down. Several of the men from the crowd stepped forward to help hold his weight while another man climbed up the crude ladder mounted on the back side of the cross, loosening first one arm and then the other. Someone on the floor unbound his feet. Wrapping the long length of fabric that had been prepared to secure him across his chest and under his arms, they carefully lowered him to the floor.

No one spoke. Every eye in the sanctuary focused on Keene. As soon as his feet touched the floor, he pulled free of the wrap and fell at the foot of the cross, his back hunched, weeping loudly and gasping for air.

Having no idea what had happened or why he asked to be taken down from the cross, Jane wanted to throw her arms around him and hold him. But instead, like everyone else on the stage, she remained motionless, confused by the scene playing out before her eyes.

&

Finally composing himself, Keene pulled himself to his knees. Every line of dialogue and every song he'd memorized while preparing for *Down from the Cross* came rushing to his mind. All thoughts of the people in the audience, the two men hanging on their crosses, his agent, his career, his future, had been set aside. Nothing else mattered except his relationship with a jealous but loving God. He, Keene Moray, was a sinner, just like Jane had said he was. Just like the Bible said he was. Why hadn't he seen it before? How could he have been so closed-minded?

Using his last bit of strength and holding on to the cross, every ounce of pride he possessed gone, Keene slowly rose to his feet, lifting his eyes heavenward. He stood there a broken man, feeling lower than the lowest and gazing at the empty cross.

Then, raising his arms high above his head, he called out in a loud voice that boomed out over the microphone, "Father, I've sinned against You! I am not worthy to portray Jesus! I can go on with this farce no longer. I am begging for Your forgiveness! Take me, God!"

A sweet peace came over him as he stood there, and he

knew God had heard his cry. He was forgiven. *Thank You, Lord. Thank You.*

Relieved and pulling himself together, he turned slowly to face the audience. He had to let those who had not yet asked God to forgive them know that God loved them and allowed Jesus to die on the cross for them, too. They had to know that they, like him, could have eternal life.

Finally, he moved away from the cross, those in front of him parting. When he reached the front of the big platform, he held out his hands to the stunned audience. "Earlier tonight, someone I love very much reminded me that the Easter story isn't just an interesting little story filled with symbolism. It is true. Every word of it. It really happened just like you have seen it portrayed here on this stage tonight. She called it the truest love story of all time. And now, thanks to God and His mercy, I know that's true."

He paused and wiped his eyes with the back of his hand. "God loved us so much He sent His only Son, Jesus, to suffer and die on the cross for sinners like me." Lifting his hand, he slowly gestured from one side of the audience to the other, pointing his finger. "And sinners like you. Don't turn your back on Him like I did. This night, I have confessed my sins to Him and asked His forgiveness. I am turning my life over to Him. From this day forth, I am His. I want Him to use me in any way He sees fit."

Turning and walking slowly back to the cross, he began to sing with great emotion a song he'd learned by listening to Jane sing it while she worked in his office.

> *"On a hill faraway stood an old rugged cross,*
> *The emblem of suffering and shame;*
> *And I love that old cross where the dearest and best*
> *For a world of lost sinners was slain."*

Kneeling at the cross and wrapping his arms around it, he continued to sing.

> *"So I'll cherish this old rugged cross,*
>   *Till my trophies at last I lay down;*
> *I will cling to the old rugged cross,*
>   *And exchange it someday for a crown."*

When he had sung the last word, Pastor Congdon stepped onto the stage and took the microphone offered to him by one of the soloists. "We've all seen a miracle here tonight. One of God's children has come into the fold. Like Keene, I am sure there are many of you who have never surrendered your heart to Christ. Do it now. Do not delay. The Savior is waiting." He bowed his head as a lone violinist stood and played "Just as I Am."

Hundreds of people thronged to the front to accept the invitation as Keene continued to hold on to the cross, weeping his heart out to his God.

Jane moved up close to him, wrapping her arm around his trembling shoulders.

Her prayers had been answered.

❧

Later that night, after closing himself up with Pastor Congdon in his office, Keene drove Jane home. Neither of them could contain their excitement as they discussed the evening's happenings.

"How could I have been so blind?" Keene asked, turning his car toward her street. "And stupid?"

Jane scooted close, as close as the console would allow, and leaned her head on his shoulder. "I don't know when I've ever been this happy, Keene. You have no idea how hard I have prayed for you. I'm sure God got tired of hearing me plead with Him to touch your heart and make you know He's real."

"Your words kept haunting me last night, and I barely got any sleep at all. Then, this evening, when you came into my dressing room—well, your concern for me really got to me."

"I didn't want to upset you, this being your last night to sing, but I wanted so much to see you get right with God before you left Rhode Island."

"Jane."

"Yes."

"I heard you last night, after the performance. I–I didn't mean to listen while you were praying, but I came back to pick up my briefcase, and there you were."

"How. . .how much did you hear?"

"All of it."

He had to smile when he turned his face from the road long enough to gaze at the rosy blush on her cheeks. "I heard you say you loved me. Did you really mean it when you told that to God?"

"I–I guess, but I didn't want you to know."

"Why?"

She sighed. "For three reasons. One, you didn't believe in God."

"I do now."

"Two. You're going to be leaving Providence before long, and I may never see you again."

"I think we can work that out. What's the third reason?"

She fidgeted in the seat before answering.

"Jane. . ."

"I knew. . .I knew you could never love me back. Not really love me, like I love you."

Without taking his attention from his driving, he leaned over and kissed the top of her head. "I learned something else tonight."

She lifted her eyes to his. "Oh? What?"

"That I do love you. Really love you."

She sat up straight and stared at him, her eyes rounding in surprise.

"I think I've loved you from that first day, but I was too stubborn to see it. You were everything I wasn't, and you made me feel guilty every time you talked about your God. I knew I was a sinner. I just didn't want you to know it. You were so pure and godly it scared me to compare myself to you."

He pulled the BMW up in front of her apartment house and turned off the engine. "Let's get out of this car. I want to hold you in my arms, and I sure don't want to have to crawl over this console." He hurried around to her side, opened the door, and held out his open arms. Jane ran into them, wrapping her arms around his strong neck when he lifted her and whirled her around. "I love you, Jane Delaney."

❧

"I love—" Before she could finish her sentence, his lips sought hers, and he held her close. Feelings of love and adoration tugged at her heart. Keene loved her! He actually loved her!

"I've wanted to kiss you like this for so long," he murmured. "Oh, I know I've kissed you before, but it wasn't the same."

She melded herself to him, reveling in his closeness. "I know. I feel the same way."

He smiled down at her. "Remember what you said a couple of nights ago? That you could never have a permanent relationship with a man who didn't share your faith?"

She gazed up at him, her heart so full she could barely remember her name. "I–I think so."

His finger touching her lip, he gave her a coy smile. "You do realize that now that I've made my peace with God, your reason number three is no longer a problem."

"Does that mean. . ."

"It means I'd like a permanent relationship with you."

She eyed him quizzically. "How. . .how permanent?"

"Like for the rest of our lives! You know. The 'M' word. Marriage. I love you. I want you to be my wife."

"Oh, Keene, as much as I'd love to marry you, I can't. At least, not now. Not yet." His frown broke her heart. "I'm not sure we would fit into one another's world."

"Jane, my dear, my beloved one, you wouldn't have to fit into my world. Don't you see? You *are* my world."

"I love you for saying that, but as much as I love you, I love Christ more. *He* is *my* world, my life, my breath. My heart tells me you are the man for me, but my head tells me we have to wait. At least for a while. You've just accepted Christ. You know so little of what it means to live for Him. You need time to grow, and we need time together. Time to really get acquainted. I want us to read the Bible together, pray together, attend church together. But how would we ever do it? You're never in one place very long."

"I'll reschedule a number of this year's singing engagements, and I'll continue to keep my office in Providence. Then once we're married, you'll be able to travel with me. We'll see the world together."

She gave her head a sad shake. "We have another problem. What about my mother? I could never go off and leave her. She's much too frail to live alone."

He appeared thoughtful. "I wouldn't want you to leave her. Your dedication to those you love is one of the things that first attracted me to you. Not many people are as concerned about their elderly parents as you are. Don't worry about it, sweetheart. We will work something out when the time comes. After all, she's going to be my mother, too, when you decide to let me place a wedding ring on your finger."

"What about—"

Pulling her quickly to him, his lips pressed hers, making it impossible for her to finish her sentence. Finally, he moved away, just enough to peer into her eyes. The love she saw there took her breath away. She smiled and was reassured when he smiled back.

"Do you honestly think God would have brought us together and put this love in our hearts for each other, and for Him, if He hadn't wanted us to be together?" Cupping her face in his hands, he asked, "Where is your faith, Jane? Or is it that you don't love me enough to want to spend your life with me?"

"My faith is strong—stronger than ever now that he has become your Savior, too. Oh, Keene. You will never know how happy it makes me to know you and I share the same faith. God has truly answered my prayers. And love you? I love you so much it hurts. Of course I want to spend my life with you! Let's just take things slowly, okay?"

He kissed her again, a sweet, tender kiss that made her fingers tingle and her toes curl. "We'll do it any way you want it." His lips still lingering, he kissed her a third time. Finally, he pulled back, his hands going to cup her shoulders, his brow bearing a slight crease. "There's something I have to tell you. Something I probably should have told you weeks ago."

The seriousness in his voice frightened her. What could be that bad? Was he going to tell her he would be leaving for New York sooner than expected? Or that he had a wife in another city?

"What?"

"Remember all those appointments I've been having lately?"

She nodded. "Yes, but you never told me what they were."

He freed one hand and rubbed at the stubble on his chin. "There was a very definite reason I chose Providence as the place I wanted to spend the months it would take me to learn the new opera. He stared off into space. "I–I. . ."

"What, Keene? You can tell me anything. I promise I'll try not to be upset."

He walked away, standing with his back to her and gazing off into the night sky, one hand kneading the muscles of his neck. "By the end of last season, I was beginning to notice periods of hoarseness. I had never had them before. They usually occurred after an exceptionally demanding performance or an unusually heavy practice day. At first I thought it might be a viral infection, but it didn't stop. I went to several doctors, but even with all the testing they did, nothing showed up, and the only advice they gave me was to get more rest and make sure I ate properly."

"But what did that have to do with Providence?"

"I'm coming to that. My voice is my livelihood. I couldn't take any chances, so I did some intense research and located a doctor in Rhode Island whose specialty is voice disorders. He was trained at Wake Forest University Baptist Medical Center where the Center for Voice Disorders is located, so the guy really knows his stuff. I've been working with him since the first week I arrived in Providence."

"Has he been able to help you?"

He turned around, facing her, crossing his long arms over his chest. "At this point, I'm not sure. At least he ruled out throat cancer. He's already done some pretty extensive testing, but until I finished singing *Down from the Cross* and could completely rest my voice for several weeks, we couldn't go ahead with a full laryngoscopy."

She stared at him. "A laryngoscopy?"

"He said by performing a laryngoscopy he would be able to detect certain types of lesions if they were present. Like nodules, cysts, papilloma, leukoplakia, and neoplasm. Wow, that's a mouthful, isn't it?"

"Could that mean surgery?"

"Maybe, maybe not. Nodules are callouslike masses that form on the vocal folds. He thinks that might be my problem. Though all singers dread them, sometimes asymptomatic vocal nodules don't seem to cause any singing problems. Usually with nodules, not only do you have hoarseness, but breathiness, loss of range, and vocal fatigue. Other than the little bit of hoarseness, I have had none of those symptoms. I have known many vocalists who had untreated vocal nodules for years and were never bothered by them. The doctor says sometimes, with vocal therapy, they will even shrink or disappear. But—"

He let out a heavy sigh, and she could tell he was trying to make the best of an extremely difficult situation.

She looped her arms about his neck. "God is able to perform miracles, Keene. We both know that."

"I know. I am counting on it, but I have to admit I was terrified when Dr. Coulter explained all this to me. Now, knowing how much God loves me, well, I can assure you I'm not nearly as frightened as I was."

"Was it wise of you to perform in our Easter presentation? And you spent so much time practicing each day, too," she said with concern now that the full extent of what he had told her had finally sunk in.

He grinned shyly. "Most of the practicing for the new opera you heard coming from my room wasn't me practicing at all, but tapes I had prerecorded of myself practicing before I got here. Since I wanted to ease up on my singing, I stayed in my room listening to the tapes and following along with the music score. I practiced my part in *Down from the Cross* the same way. I recorded it once and then mouthed it over and over until I'd learned the part."

"I never knew!"

"That's what I was counting on. I didn't want you to worry

about me." Taking both her hands in his, he gave them a loving squeeze. "When you came to me, asking me to take Jim Carter's place, I didn't want to have to tell you no. And I certainly didn't want to tell you what I would be facing in the future. I knew if I did, you would never allow me to sing the part of Jesus, and I wanted to sing that part, not just for you, but also for myself. I had never done anything quite like it, and I thought the experience would be a good professional stretch for me. Dr. Coulter said that since I would only be singing several songs and my speaking parts would be limited, it would not hurt to put both the resting period and tests off until after Easter. So it looks like I'm going to be in Providence for a while after all."

"I was so afraid you'd leave right away."

"You do realize the laryngoscopy may show there are other problems, problems that could be even more serious than a simple node. I don't even want to talk about those, but I do want you to be prepared, sweetheart. There is always the possibility that Dr. Coulter will discover something that will require extensive surgery. If that happens, Jane—"

She held her breath.

"If that happens, I may never be able to sing again. The vocal cords and folds are easily damaged during surgery. There are no guarantees." He blinked and swallowed hard. "My career would be over, and I'd be washed up. Out of a job. I would have to start all over again. Learn a new trade." His finger idly traced her cheek, his expression one of sadness. "Never be able to sing to my wife."

Jane couldn't help but gasp. Never be able to sing again? *Oh, dear Father. No! Surely, You won't let this happen to Keene!*

"Other than my doctor, you're the only one I've told. My agent doesn't even know."

She had to do something, say something, to comfort him.

Forcing a smile, she cradled his face in her hands and kissed his lips. "Oh, my darling, don't you know? It's not your voice I love. It's you! We'll see this thing through together, and no matter what the outcome, God will take care of us. You'll see."

"I know that's true, my sweet, sweet Jane. I am at peace about this whole thing now. I have put it in God's hands. I am trusting in Him and His promises. I want His perfect will for my life. Even. . .even if it means giving up singing."

"He's able to do above all we could ever ask. We have to trust Him."

"I know that now. With God in control of my life and you at my side, I can face anything. I know very little about the things of God. It's all new to me, but I want to learn everything about God and His Word. I am sure there will be times I will need your strength and encouragement to help me through, Jane, but I want to be strong for you—the husband you deserve. With God's help, I will be."

"I will be at your side, Keene, for as long as I live. God intended a wife to be a helpmeet to her husband. He will never leave you, and neither will I."

"Does that mean you love me enough to want to spend the rest of your life as my wife? That there'll be a wedding in our future?"

She gazed up into his eyes, her heart crowding her chest with love for this man. The man she would have dared not believe could one day love her as much as she loved him. "Oh, yes, my dearest. Loving you and knowing you love me is a dream come true."

"For me, too, Jane. I can't praise God enough for bringing you into my life."

epilogue

Jane Moray sat twisting the lovely diamond wedding band on the ring finger of her left hand. "Mom, can you believe it's been almost a year since our wedding day?"

Mrs. Delaney smiled at her daughter. "It thrills my heart to see you and Keene so happy."

"Isn't he wonderful?" Jane asked as they sat on a front pew of Fort Worth's spacious Briarwood Community Church. "The Lord has really been able to use Keene in a mighty way since his horrendous throat problems. Only God could have guided Dr. Coulter's hand and protected Keene's vocal cords during that intense surgery."

Mrs. Delaney grasped her daughter's hand in hers. "Yes, Keene *is* wonderful. He is like the son I never had and always wanted, and he has taken such good care of me. Without him, I never would have been able to afford to have my knees replaced. Now look at me. I can walk without my walker, and I am able to take care of myself while you two go traipsing around the world to all the exotic places where Keene performs. I have a nice place to live only minutes away from your lovely house in Providence, friends to keep me company, and a daughter and son-in-law whom I adore. God has blessed me more abundantly than I ever could have imagined."

Jane patted her mother's frail hand. "You know, Mom, the day Keene ran that red light and plowed into me with that heavy car of his, I thought God had forsaken me. The whole side of my little car was caved in, I had a broken leg and a massive bump on my head, was three months behind in my car and insurance payments, out of a job, and I had no idea where the next month's rent money was coming from or if we'd have food on our table. Now we have a beautiful home, and I'm able to travel with my dear husband as he performs in the opera and gives concerts." She gave her mother's small hand another loving pat. "God is good, isn't He? He has certainly provided well for our needs."

Mrs. Delaney leaned into her daughter, her face twisted into a mischievous grin. "Maybe someday you'll fill up that beautiful house with my grandchildren."

Jane could not contain her smile as her palm flattened against her belly. "Maybe."

"Don't wait too long, honey. I want to be around to enjoy them."

"I won't, I promise. Keene loves performing as a Christian artist, and he's already contracted to produce several albums over the next few years."

"Oh, my, how can he take on so many projects? Won't that mean he'll be away from home even more?"

Jane smiled broadly. "No, in fact, he's already talking about retiring from opera. Other than the Christian concerts he'll be doing, he will spend most of his time at home learning new songs and preparing for his recordings." Jane glanced at the podium then put a finger to her lips. "Shh. It's time for his concert to begin."

The pastor moved to the microphone, surveying the crowded sanctuary. "We're so glad to have you here with us tonight. You are in for a real treat. The name Keene Moray is known all over the world. Keene is a professional and at the peak of his career. But a little over a year ago, God spoke to his heart, and Keene accepted Christ as his Savior. Now a major portion of his time is spent giving concerts like the one you'll be hearing tonight." Gesturing toward Keene, he said,

"Ladies and gentlemen, it is my honor and privilege to introduce to you. . .Keene Moray."

With an adoring glance toward his wife, Keene rose and stepped to the front of the platform. "Thank you, Pastor. But before I begin, I must introduce my wonderful, supportive wife. Jane, would you stand, please?"

She stood and waved to the crowd.

"And with Jane is her mother, Lutie Delaney."

His mother-in-law turned and smiled at the audience.

"If it weren't for Jane and her patient and consistent witness to me," he went on, "I wouldn't be here tonight. Her prayers are what brought me to a saving knowledge of Christ. Thank you, sweetheart."

Jane blew him a kiss. Though Keene always introduced her and said the same sweet things about her, she never tired of hearing them.

"Much of the music I'll be performing tonight is from an Easter pageant. Its words and music, plus the prayers of Jane and the other members of Randlewood Community Church in Providence, Rhode Island, are what brought me into God's fold."

He paused, and Jane knew he was remembering that night.

"A little over a year ago, I was invited to sing the part of Jesus in the Easter pageant *Down from the Cross*. At the time, I did not believe God existed. But through singing the part of Jesus and realizing the suffering He endured to take my sins upon Him and die on the cross, I knew I was a sinner and wanted to be saved."

Keene pulled out his handkerchief and wiped at his eyes. "On the final night of the pageant, Easter night, as I hung on that cross, I realized I was a sinner and unworthy to portray the Son of God. I frantically asked the soldiers to take me down. I could not bear to hang there a minute longer. When they stood me to my feet, I fell at the foot of the cross and asked God to forgive me of my sins and accept me into His family."

He bowed his head, his chest heaving silently. When he finally looked up at the audience, tears were streaming down his ruddy face. "I implore each of you: If you have not accepted Christ, do it tonight. Don't put it off like I did."

He nodded to his accompanist, and she began to play.

"Please, listen to the words. Let them touch your heart as they touched mine that night, over a year ago, when I came 'down from the cross' to accept my Lord."

A Letter To Our Readers

Dear Reader:

In order that we might better contribute to your reading enjoyment, we would appreciate your taking a few minutes to respond to the following questions. We welcome your comments and read each form and letter we receive. When completed, please return to the following:

Fiction Editor
Heartsong Presents
PO Box 719
Uhrichsville, Ohio 44683

1. Did you enjoy reading *Down from the Cross* by Joyce Livingston?
   ❑ Very much! I would like to see more books by this author!
   ❑ Moderately. I would have enjoyed it more if

   _____
   _____
   _____

2. Are you a member of **Heartsong Presents**? ❑ Yes ❑ No
   If no, where did you purchase this book? _____
   _____

3. How would you rate, on a scale from 1 (poor) to 5 (superior), the cover design? _____

4. On a scale from 1 (poor) to 10 (superior), please rate the following elements.

   ____ Heroine   ____ Plot
   ____ Hero   ____ Inspirational theme
   ____ Setting   ____ Secondary characters

5. These characters were special because?_____

_____

_____

6. How has this book inspired your life?_____

_____

_____

7. What settings would you like to see covered in future
   Heartsong Presents books? _____

_____

_____

8. What are some inspirational themes you would like to see
   treated in future books? _____

_____

_____

9. Would you be interested in reading other **Heartsong
   Presents** titles? ❏ Yes ❏ No

10. Please check your age range:
    ❏ Under 18   ❏ 18-24
    ❏ 25-34   ❏ 35-45
    ❏ 46-55   ❏ Over 55

Name _____

Occupation _____

Address _____

City_____ State_____ Zip_____

$\mathcal{A}$LABAMA

4 stories in 1

$\mathcal{N}$estled in the northeastern mountains of Alabama is the fictional town of Rockdale. The small Southern town has become a haven for four women who have given up on finding love.

Four complete inspirational romance stories by author Kay Cornelius.

Contemporary, paperback, 480 pages, 5 ³/₁₆" x 8"

❤ ❤ ❤ ❤ ❤ ❤ ❤ ❤ ❤ ❤ ❤ ❤ ❤ ❤ ❤ ❤

❤ ❤ ❤ ❤ ❤ ❤ ❤ ❤ ❤ ❤ ❤ ❤ ❤ ❤ ❤ ❤

Presents

Great Inspirational Romance at a Great Price!

Heartsong Presents books are inspirational romances in contemporary and historical settings, designed to give you an enjoyable, spirit-lifting reading experience. You can choose wonderfully written titles from some of today's best authors like Hannah Alexander, Andrea Boeshaar, Yvonne Lehman, Tracie Peterson, and many others.

When ordering quantities less than twelve, above titles are $2.97 each.
Not all titles may be available at time of order.

$\mathcal{H}$EARTSONG ❤ PRESENTS

Love Stories Are Rated G!

That's for godly, gratifying, and of course, great! If you love a thrilling love story but don't appreciate the sordidness of some popular paperback romances, **Heartsong Presents** is for you. In fact, **Heartsong Presents** is the premiere inspirational romance book club featuring love stories where Christian faith is the primary ingredient in a marriage relationship.

Sign up today to receive your first set of four, never-before-published Christian romances. Send no money now; you will receive a bill with the first shipment. You may cancel at any time without obligation, and if you aren't completely satisfied with any selection, you may return the books for an immediate refund!

Imagine. . .four new romances every four weeks—two historical, two contemporary—with men and women like you who long to meet the one God has chosen as the love of their lives. . .all for the low price of $10.99 postpaid.

To join, simply complete the coupon below and mail to the address provided. **Heartsong Presents** romances are rated G for another reason: They'll arrive Godspeed!

YES! Sign me up for Heart❤ng!

NEW MEMBERSHIPS WILL BE SHIPPED IMMEDIATELY!
Send no money now. We'll bill you only $10.99 post-paid with your first shipment of four books. Or for faster action, call toll free 1-800-847-8270.

NAME _____

ADDRESS _____

CITY_____ STATE_____ ZIP_____

MAIL TO: HEARTSONG PRESENTS, P.O. Box 721, Uhrichsville, Ohio 44683
or visit www.heartsongpresents.com